Teddy Roosevelt

Young Rough Rider
By Edd Winfield Parks

Aladdin Paperbacks

Aladdin Paperbacks
An imprint of Simon & Schuster
Children's Publishing Division
1230 Avenue of the Americas
New York, NY 10020
Copyright © 1953, 1961 by the Bobbs-Merrill Company, Inc.
All rights reserved including the right of reproduction
in whole or in part in any form.
First Aladdin Paperbacks edition, 1989
Printed in the United States of America

20   19   18   17   16   15   14   13   12   11

Library of Congress Cataloging-in-Publication Data
Parks, Edd Winfield, 1906–1968.
Teddy Roosevelt: young rough rider/by Edd Winfield Parks. —
1st Aladdin Books ed.
          p.   cm.
Reprint. Originally published: Teddy Roosevelt: all-round boy.
Indianapolis: Bobbs-Merrill, 1953.
Summary: Focuses on the childhood of the dynamic president,
describing how Teddy worked hard to improve his poor health and
developed a lifelong interest in nature and the conservation of
natural resources.
ISBN 0-689-71349-5
1. Roosevelt, Theodore, 1858–1919—Childhood and youth—Juvenile
literature.   2. Presidents—United States—Biography—Juvenile
literature.   [1. Roosevelt, Theodore, 1858–1919—Childhood and
youth.   2. Presidents.]   I. Title.
E757.P25   1989
973.91'1'092—dc20
[B]   [92]   89-37819   CIP   AC

To Sherrill, Harry Edward, Janie,
Peggy, and David

Illustrations

Full pages

Numerous smaller illustrations

Contents

★ ★ # Teddy

Roosevelt

Young Rough Rider

The Birthday

MR. ROOSEVELT was driving two fine black horses at a fast pace. Their iron shoes rang on the cobblestones of the New York City street.

Theodore sat up straight by his father's side. His wool coat was buttoned up tightly. The October wind was getting cold.

"This drive has been exciting," he said. "It's the best birthday present you could give me."

Mr. Roosevelt looked down at his eight-year-old son and smiled.

"Birthdays are so much fun. I can hardly wait to open my presents at home," Theodore remarked happily.

"It's been fun for me, too," Mr. Roosevelt said. "And it's been fun for your visiting cousins, Johnnie and Maud Elliott."

Johnnie and Maud had come from Georgia that summer to make a long visit with their aunt, Theodore's mother. They were still visiting on Theodore's birthday, October 27, 1866.

"Whoa, Boone! Whoa, Crockett!" The horses slowed down. Mr. Roosevelt stopped them alongside a newsboy standing on the corner. "I'll take a paper, Mike." He pulled a coin out of his pocket. "How are you?"

"Fine, thank you, sir," Mike answered cheerfully. "It's a little chilly, though."

Theodore saw that the newsboy's hands and face were red and chapped from the cold. His jacket was ragged. He didn't have an overcoat.

"Mike, this is my son Theodore. He's coming to the Newsboys' Dinner next Sunday night. I hope you're coming, too."

12

Mike stuck out a cold, dirty hand. "Pleased to meet you, Teddy," he said and grinned.

Theodore shook hands warmly. He grinned back, showing his big white teeth. "You'll have to show me the ropes Sunday night." He liked the looks of Mike's pleasant, freckled face.

"The food is wonderful," said Mike. "Mr. Roosevelt always sees to it that we have a good time."

"I'll see you there, Mike," said Theodore.

His father clucked to the horses. "Get up, Boone and Crockett! Good-by, Mike. Don't forget us."

"You bet your life I won't," Mike called after them.

Mr. Roosevelt drove to his house on East Twentieth Street. "You go on in. I'll take the horses to the livery stable."

Theodore's mother opened the door. "Hurry back, Theodore," she called to her husband.

Then she leaned over and kissed her son. "And did this Theodore have a good time?"

"Yes'm, I sure did. I saw the Hudson River steamboats, and we rode out in the country ever so fast."

"Come into the parlor," said Mrs. Roosevelt. "I have a special surprise for you." She opened the door to the room.

The big gas chandelier with its gleaming glass made him blink. Then Theodore saw his grandparents, Mr. and Mrs. Cornelius Roosevelt, sitting on a horsehair sofa. "Grandfather and Grandmother! How nice of you to come!" He hugged them both.

He greeted the other older members of his family. Aunt Anna, Mother's sister, who taught him his lessons, was there. Sitting next to her were Uncle Rob and Aunt Elizabeth Roosevelt, who lived next door. Grandmother Bulloch stood beside Aunt Elizabeth.

"Why, it's a big party!" he cried, delighted.

His grandfather held out a large package. "This is for you. Take it upstairs, where the other children are. They will enjoy seeing you open it."

Grandmother Bulloch smiled at him. "I have something, too, but I want you to open it here. I want to see if it fits."

Theodore eagerly tore off the red ribbon and the green wrapping paper. He held up a dark-blue coat with shining brass buttons. "Gee, it's beautiful!" he gasped with delight. Quickly he took off his old gray coat and put on the new one.

Grandmother Bulloch looked at it closely. "It may be a little big, but you'll grow up to it soon."

"Oh, yes! Thank you very much, Grandmother." Theodore walked proudly around the room. Suddenly he stopped. He was thinking hard. "Grandmother," he said, going up to her, "I met a mighty nice newsboy today. His name is Mike.

16

He's a little bigger than I am. It would fit him exactly, and he doesn't have a coat. Would you mind if I gave it to him?"

Grandmother Bulloch looked both pleased and disturbed. "I like to have you think of other people," she said slowly. "Maybe you don't like the coat?"

"I like it better than any coat I've ever had," Theodore protested quickly. "But I remember how cold Mike was, out in the wind."

His mother spoke firmly. "No, Theodore. I'm proud of your thoughtfulness, but you mustn't give away things people have given you. You can give him the coat you just took off. That will keep him just as warm."

"Bully!" said Theodore. "Now Mike and I will both have coats. I'd hate to give away Grandmother's present."

"Now run upstairs and open your other gifts," said his mother. "Take your new coat with you."

Theodore went straight to the upstairs playroom. Other presents were waiting for him on a table in the center of the room. His older sister Anna was in one corner reading. His brother Elliott, only a year younger than he, and his four-year-old sister Corinne were playing jack-stones with their three cousins—Johnnie and Maud Elliott and John Ellis Roosevelt.

Maud and Corinne (Conie for short) were the same age. Johnnie, Theodore, and John Ellis were all eight years old.

John Ellis was Uncle Rob's son. Everybody called him Jack. He handed Theodore a flat, square package. "I brought you a picture book of animals," he said.

"Gee!" exclaimed Theodore. "It's a beauty."

"Let's see what else you got," said Conie impatiently.

Theodore laid the book carefully on the table and began opening the other packages.

"Toy soldiers from Grandfather," he cried delightedly. "And a toy ship from Uncle Rob and Aunt Elizabeth, and—Make a list of them for me, will you please, Johnnie? I'll call them off as I open them."

Just as they finished exclaiming over the presents, Aunt Anna Bulloch came in. "Look at all I got, Aunt Anna," Theodore called.

"Splendid!" she said, smiling. "But dinner is ready now. You may play with your gifts after you have eaten."

As they started down the stairs, Johnnie Elliott said, "Here's your list, Theodore. You'll know just whom to thank for what."

"Thanks, Johnnie."

Then Johnnie said teasingly, "What kind of a boy are you, anyhow? I've been wondering about that as I wrote the names down. Your grandpapa Roosevelt is a Dutchman. Your grandmother Roosevelt is English. Your grandmother Bulloch is Scotch. Your papa's a New Yorker, and your mama's from Georgia. Just what does that make you?" Johnnie grinned in delight. He thought he had his cousin stumped.

The older people were waiting at the bottom of the stairs. They heard this teasing.

Theodore stopped. "I'll tell you what it makes me," he said proudly. "It makes me a one-hundred-percent American!"

Johnnie had no answer to that.

Grandfather Roosevelt smiled broadly. He said, "That's the spirit, Theodore! I'm proud of being a Dutchman, but I'm most proud of being an American."

"Yes, sir, I am, too," said Theodore.

THE NEWSBOYS' DINNER

The next Sunday evening Theodore went with Mr. Roosevelt to the Newsboys' Lodginghouse.

Theodore was wearing his new blue coat with the brass buttons. He carried his old gray coat over his arm to give to Mike.

Mr. Charles Brace, one of Mr. Roosevelt's friends, greeted them. "The boys will be delighted to see you, Mr. Roosevelt. I'm glad you came too, Theodore." Mr. Brace, like Theodore's father, went often to the Newsboys' Lodging-house.

"I'm going to come often," Theodore said with enthusiasm. "Where's Mike Brady?"

"He's over there singing," Mr. Brace answered.

One boy was playing "The Old Oaken Bucket" on the piano. Other boys, grouped behind him, were singing lustily——

"The old oaken bucket, the iron-bound
        bucket,
    The moss-covered bucket which hung
        in the well."

Theodore sang, too.

He saw Mike's freckled face. "Hey, Mike!" he yelled joyfully when the song was ended.

"Gee!" Mike cried. "It's Teddy Roosevelt!" He came forward, grinning.

"I brought you something, Mike." Teddy held out the gray coat.

Mike looked at it unbelievingly. "Why, it's a beauty! But I can't take it. You'll need it."

Theodore fingered the brass buttons on his new coat. "Grandmother Bulloch gave me this for my birthday. I was going to give it to you, but Mother said that wouldn't be polite to Grandmother."

Mike put the gray coat on proudly. "Gee! Thanks, Teddy." The coat fitted well on his thin shoulders.

"Dinner is ready, boys," said Mr. Brace, coming up to them.

Theodore met all the boys. He ate roast beef, mashed potatoes, and gravy. After dinner he joined heartily in the games. He enjoyed every minute he was with Mike and the other boys.

As Teddy and his father were getting ready to leave, Mike asked anxiously, "Are you sure you don't want the gray coat, Teddy?"

"I'm sure, Mike. I'll be seeing you."

When they were outside, on the sidewalk, Mr. Roosevelt asked, "Did you have a good time, Theodore?"

"I sure did! It's a funny thing, Father. Nobody at home calls me Teddy, but Mike and all the boys here do." He thought a moment. "It's a good name," he added.

Little Rough Rider

"I LIKE the country," said Teddy. "I like the green trees and shady dirt roads. Even the air smells fresher. I don't ever want to go back to New York, Bamie."

"I do," said his sister Anna. Everyone called her "Bamie." She was four years older than Teddy. "I like New York City better than any other place in the world. You're just too young to like it."

"I'm eight and a half," her brother told her hotly.

"We'll spend the summer here," said Mrs. Roosevelt. "Now you must stay quiet, Theodore.

The doctor said for you to lie down for an hour after lunch every day."

"I'll bet I've been here more than an hour." Teddy was lying on a cot on the front porch. "I want to go play with Ellie and Conie. I haven't had asthma in a long time."

"We don't want you to have it at all," said his mother. "You rest ten minutes longer. Then you can go play."

The Roosevelt family was spending the summer of 1867 in New Jersey. Mr. Roosevelt had rented a large farmhouse. He wanted his children to be outdoors as much as possible.

"We've been here a week," said Teddy. "I've already seen a green heron, a kingbird, a red-winged blackbird, and a——"

Bamie interrupted him. "You told Papa at breakfast that you'd seen thirty-nine different kinds of birds. Are you going to name all of them?" she asked in a teasing voice.

"He could do it," said Mrs. Roosevelt proudly. "I know he could."

"I wonder where Papa is? I've seen forty-two kinds of birds now—three more since breakfast. I want to tell him about the new ones."

"He said he might be gone all day," his mother answered.

Ellie and Conie came running around the corner of the house.

"Papa's coming," said Conie importantly. "We were in the hayloft in the barn and we saw his buggy."

"And guess what?" Ellie shouted. "There is a baby horse following after the buggy."

A few moments later Mr. Roosevelt drove up in front of the house. He stopped his horse and got out of the buggy. "Come see what I have, children."

Teddy jumped up excitedly. "What's that behind the buggy, Papa?"

Mr. Roosevelt smiled. "It's a pony for all of you." He hurried to the rear of the buggy and untied the pony. As he led it toward the porch, he said, "His name is General Grant."

Conie was dancing up and down excitedly. Teddy and Ellie ran toward the small, reddish-brown pony. Teddy shouted, "He has a saddle and bridle. He's all ready to ride."

The pony started to back away.

"Easy, Theodore," said his father. "You must go up to a horse quietly."

The boy stopped. "He's the handsomest pony I ever saw. Isn't he a beauty, Ellie? May I pat him, Papa? I won't scare him." He approached the pony slowly and patted him on the forehead. General Grant stood very still. Ellie came up and put one hand on the pony's mane.

"Thank you, Papa," Theodore said. "This pony is just what we have always wanted. May I ride him now?"

"I want to ride first," said Conie. "He's my Pony Grant, too."

"Come here. You're the littlest, so you get to ride first." Mr. Roosevelt lifted her onto the pony's back. Holding the bridle, he walked the pony around in a circle.

"When I ride him I want to gallop," said Teddy.

"You can't do that today," said his father. "General Grant has trotted eight miles already. You can make him gallop tomorrow."

"Whee-ee-ee!" Conie leaned over and patted the pony's neck. "I'm just going to love you, Pony Grant."

RIDING GENERAL GRANT

Teddy got up bright and early the next morning. When he went downstairs, he found his father walking in the front yard.

"I'm ready to ride General Grant," said Teddy.

"What! Before breakfast?"

"Yes, sir. Right now."

"Can you put a saddle and bridle on him?"

"I don't know, but I'm going to try."

Mr. Roosevelt smiled at his son. "I'll help you. But I want you to learn to take care of him yourself. Wait. I'll get a lump of sugar. You must make friends with the General."

In the barn Teddy held the lump of sugar under the pony's mouth. General Grant sniffed at Teddy's hand. Then his soft, moist, warm tongue licked at the sugar.

"Gee, he sure likes it!" Teddy exclaimed.

"He likes apples, too. Give him one tomorrow." Mr. Roosevelt lifted the bridle from a peg on the wall. "Hold it so you can put the bit between his teeth."

Teddy took the bridle. With his left hand he started to put the bit in the pony's mouth.

General Grant turned his head away. Teddy felt very clumsy, but he was determined to do the work himself. With his right hand he pulled the pony's head toward him.

"That's right," said Mr. Roosevelt. "Rub the bit between his lips. He'll open his teeth."

The bit slipped easily into the pony's mouth. Teddy pushed the bridle behind the pony's ears. "That wasn't so hard," he said. He got the saddle blanket and the saddle.

"Be sure you have the blanket on smoothly," said his father. "You can't ride a horse that has a sore back."

Teddy smoothed the blanket on General Grant's back. Then he placed the saddle on it. He reached under the pony for the cinch and pulled the strap tight before he buckled it.

Mr. Roosevelt felt the saddle. "That isn't tight enough, Theodore." He pulled the cinch tighter. "Now—that will do."

Teddy patted General Grant's forehead. Then he led him out into the barnyard. He moved around to the pony's right side.

"That's the wrong side," said Mr. Roosevelt. "You put the saddle and bridle on so well I thought you knew about mounting a horse. Always get on from the left side."

"But I'm right-handed," Teddy protested.

"If you mount from the left, then you have your right hand free."

Teddy walked to the other side. He put his left hand on the saddle and took the reins in his right hand. Then he put his left foot in the stirrup.

"Do you want me to help you?" asked his father.

"No, sir. I want to do it myself," Teddy replied. Awkwardly he flung his right leg over the pony's back and tried to get his right foot into the stirrup.

General Grant stood still for a moment, but his legs stiffened under him.

Suddenly the pony bucked. Teddy's feet were jerked out of the stirrups. His hands clutched desperately at the saddle.

General Grant bucked again. Teddy sailed through the air. He landed face down.

He scrambled to his feet and looked at the pony. General Grant was calmly watching him.

"Are you hurt, son?" asked Mr. Roosevelt.

Teddy wiggled his shoulders. "No, sir. I'm all right." He was shaking a little, but he forced himself to walk back to the pony's left side.

"No, son. Don't get on him again. Mr. Smith told me he was gentle. I'll take him back today."

Teddy turned. His lips were pressed tightly together. "I must ride him, Papa. I won't let a pony beat me. I must ride him."

Mr. Roosevelt hesitated. At last he said, "Well, try it once more."

Teddy grasped the saddle tightly. This time he'd be ready. The pony stiffened but stood quietly. Teddy swung into the saddle.

General Grant started to buck. Teddy pulled hard on the reins. He had his feet securely in the stirrups.

"Get up, General!" he yelled excitedly.

General Grant tried to get his head down. Teddy pulled harder on the reins. The pony bucked once more, but Teddy held on grimly.

The pony leaped forward. His legs were still stiff. He jolted Teddy up and down, but Teddy guided the pony around the barn.

Mr. Roosevelt watched anxiously. When General Grant came in sight again, he was running smoothly.

"Whee!" Teddy gasped. "That was a rough ride." He rode around the barn again.

The boy stopped the pony in front of his father. "General Grant's all right now. Please open the barn gate, Papa. I want really to ride him—a long way."

Mr. Roosevelt thought it over. "Be careful, son," he cautioned, as he opened the gate.

"Yippee!" shouted Teddy.

General Grant started running very fast down the lane toward the main road.

Later General Grant trotted up to the front porch. Teddy sat proudly in the saddle.

Mr. and Mrs. Roosevelt walked quickly down the steps. "We've been so worried about you," said Teddy's mother.

"Did he throw you again?" asked his father.

Teddy saw Ellie, Conie, and Bamie watching him. He sat up very straight in the saddle. "No, sir. I rode all the way to Four Corners and back. He's a wonderful pony."

"He's hard to ride, though. He likes to throw his rider," said Mr. Roosevelt. "I don't know whether we ought to keep him."

"You must keep him, Papa," pleaded Teddy, "because I want to take a long ride before breakfast every morning."

"Teedie can ride him." Conie looked at her brother proudly. "And I'm going to ride him, too." She started toward the pony.

37

"You can't ride him until you learn to say 'Teddy' plainly," Teddy teased her.

"Not right now, Conie," said her father, smiling. "Take him to the barn, Theodore, unsaddle and water him."

"Hurry, Theodore. Your breakfast is waiting," Mrs. Roosevelt called.

Teddy looked at his father. "You'll keep him?" he begged.

Mr. Roosevelt nodded and smiled. "We'll all keep him. You were thrown, but you didn't let it scare you."

"I was scared," Teddy confessed. "I just acted as if I wasn't."

"That's even better," said Mr. Roosevelt. "The next time you won't be scared at all."

Teddy clucked to the pony and started for the barn. "Yippee!" he shouted. "I'm a rough and tough rider."

The Roosevelt Museum

A LITTLE over a year later Theodore was lying on his stomach in the library of the Roosevelts' New York house, looking at a big book. He liked to look at pictures of big animals. This time he was looking at a huge whale. He had come downstairs very early in the morning.

"Theodore," his mother called. "Theodore!" Her soft voice grew louder. She came to the door. "I called you, Theodore."

He scrambled to his feet. "I didn't hear you, Mother. I'm sorry."

"You never hear anything when you have your nose in a book. Now run down to the market—

to Antonio's—and get some fresh strawberries. Come straight back. We want the strawberries for breakfast."

Teddy smiled. His teeth were big and white. "Yes, Mother."

"Tell Antonio to charge them."

Teddy ran out of the library and through the hall. He jumped down the front steps.

A wagon loaded with barrels was going by. Four big horses pulled it slowly along.

"Hello," Teddy called to the driver.

"Morning," the driver called back. "You want a ride, little boy?"

Nine-year-old Teddy didn't like to be called little. "You go too slow. I like fast horses."

He ran down the street. The wagon creaked behind him. Teddy turned the corner. He hurried on until he arrived at the city market.

He came first to the fish stall. He liked to look at the fish with ice packed around them. Some were red; some were black; but more of them were speckled.

Today Mr. Murphy had a new fish. It was very big and very black. It lay on a wooden table. There wasn't any ice around it.

Teddy walked close to it. "Why, that's a seal," he said. He had never seen a seal before, but it looked just like the picture in his book. Close up he saw that it was yellowish-gray with many dark-brown spots.

"Ugly-looking beast, isn't it?" came a voice from the doorway. Teddy jerked around and saw Mr. Murphy, the big, fat Irishman. Mr. Murphy smiled good-naturedly.

"I like it," said Teddy. "I wish it was mine."

"What would you do with it?"

"I'm going to start a collection," Teddy answered slowly. "I've collected some stamps, but I'd rather have birds and beasts and fish."

"It would smell terrible in a couple of days.

Your mother wouldn't like it. Say, did she send you for some fish for breakfast?"

"No, sir, for strawberries. I'd better get them right now."

He hated to leave the seal. It was bigger than he was. He looked at it once more. Right after breakfast he'd come back.

BR'ER RABBIT

Teddy pushed back his chair from the breakfast table. "I'm going to see Cousin Jimmy," he told his mother.

"All right," said Mrs. Roosevelt, "but don't forget to say good morning to your aunt and uncle. I've never seen you eat in such a hurry."

"I want to go with you, Teedie," said little Corinne.

"Not today, Conie. I have to see Jimmy on business."

"I guess I can go," said Elliott.

Teddy frowned. He didn't want to be bothered with the younger children today.

"You coughed all last night, Ellie," he said. "I'm usually the one who does that. And then Mother makes me stay in the house."

"I want to go," Conie whimpered.

Mrs. Roosevelt smiled at her children. "Now run along, Theodore. Elliott, you and Corinne go upstairs with Aunt Anna. She'll tell you a story about Br'er Rabbit." Mother knew how Theodore loved stories about animals.

Teddy hesitated. He'd like to hear the story, too. But someone might buy the seal from Mr. Murphy. "Won't you tell me that story tonight, Aunt Anna?" he pleaded.

His aunt smiled at him. She was young and pretty, and she spoke in a soft Southern voice. "You can't have everything, Theodore. Listen to the story now, or you may not get to hear it.

I know lots of Br'er Rabbit stories, but if you leave you won't get to hear them."

Teddy scratched his head. Then he made up his mind. "Maybe you'll tell it to me the next time I have asthma," he said, smiling at his aunt. "This business is terribly important."

MEASURING THE SEAL

Teddy pointed to the seal. "See, Jimmy," he said excitedly.

"Gee, Teddy!" Jimmy Roosevelt exclaimed. "It's a whopper, isn't it?"

"I'll say it is." Teddy pulled a tape measure out of his pocket. He had borrowed it from his mother. "I'm going to measure this big fellow." He stretched the tape along the seal and counted off the number of feet. "Why, it's over six feet long! This seal is longer than Papa is tall."

Teddy dropped the tape measure. He took a

pencil and notebook out of his pocket. Carefully he printed the word "SEAL" at the top of the page. Under that word he wrote the word "length," and added, "6 feet, 1½ inches."

"Now," he said to Jimmy, "you hold it up while I slip the tape under to measure around it."

"I don't want to," said Jimmy. "It looks dirty and slimy to me."

"You're planning to be a doctor, aren't you?"

"You bet I am," Jimmy answered, "but I'm not planning to doctor seals."

"Well, a doctor's a scientist," Teddy argued, "and we're doing this for the sake of science. You just can't refuse to lift this seal up."

Jimmy hesitated. He didn't want to put his hands on it. "There's no place to catch hold," he objected.

Mr. Murphy had finished weighing a fish for a customer. He stood listening to the boys. "Wait a minute," he said. "I'll lift it for you."

"That will be better, Teddy," said Jimmy. "He can hold it steady."

"Yes, but you're the one who's going to be a doctor. You're the one who should do it."

Mr. Murphy put his big hands under the seal.

He lifted it a little. Then he grunted. "Hurry up," he said. "This thing is heavy and slippery."

Quickly Teddy put his tape under the seal.

The seal slipped in Mr. Murphy's hands. "Hurry!" he said again.

Teddy bent close over the tape measure. "It's eleven inches on the bottom, I think," he said. He pulled the tape out. "That's close enough, anyway. Thank you, Mr. Murphy." He went on measuring. "It's three feet around where it's biggest."

"You're mighty interested in that seal," said Mr. Murphy.

"Of course I am," Teddy said. "I need one for my collection. How much money do you want for it?"

"A penny a pound. That'll make the price one or two dollars. It's just a harbor seal. The hide is no good for fur, but it could be used for something."

Theodore was disappointed. He looked hopefully at Jimmy.

"I have exactly one nickel and one penny, Teddy."

"I have a dime and three pennies," Teddy added. "That's not enough."

"You couldn't do anything with this seal," said Mr. Murphy. "It would soon rot. But I'll tell you what I'll do. I'll sell the blubber to the candlemaker early tomorrow morning. He can make candles out of the fat. Then I'll sell the hide to the trunkmaker. Since neither of them is likely to want the head, though, I'll save the head for you."

Teddy wanted to dance up and down. Instead, he answered seriously, "That will be wonderful. The head will be the finest thing in the Roosevelt Museum."

"But you don't have a museum," Jimmy objected strongly.

"Yes, I have too. I started it this minute. It's going to be the Roosevelt Museum of Natural History." He turned to the big Irishman. "You've done a lot for it. I'm going to print a card and put it right by the seal's head. It will tell everybody the head is the gift of Mr. Murphy to the museum."

"You come back tomorrow and get it," said Mr. Murphy. "You're welcome to it, even without that fine card."

"I say, Teddy, may I belong to this museum with you?" Jimmy asked.

Teddy looked undecided. "I want you to belong, Jimmy. A doctor really ought to. But next time you'll have to help me more. It's important for you to learn."

"I will," said Jimmy. "I promise. What are you going to have in your museum?"

"Well, anything that's natural history—birds and bird nests, fish, animals, animal bones."

Jimmy was getting excited. "Say, maybe we'd better get Jack to join the museum. His father has promised him a big stuffed salmon."

Teddy nodded. "Uncle Rob is a Roosevelt, too, so Cousin Jack would be all right. But we don't want too many people in it."

"That's right," agreed Jimmy.

"Just you and me, and maybe Jack." Teddy thought a moment. Then he said with determination, "I'll tell you what! We'll make the Roosevelt Museum of Natural History the best one in New York City."

The Unusual Toad

TEDDY and his cousin Jimmy came out of the Dutch Reformed church together. Sunday school was just over.

"I guess the big people have gone home," said Jimmy. "Do you want to wait for Ellie and Conie?"

"They're at home with Aunt Anna," said Teddy. "Ellie was sick last night. He ate three pieces of chicken, two hunks of cake, and every bit of rock candy we had. Then he couldn't understand why he was sick at his stomach."

"You didn't get a bite of candy?"

"No," Teddy answered. "Ellie found it first."

He thought about what Ellie had done. "I guess that's why I'm not sick."

Teddy and Jimmy started walking home. They didn't like to go along Broadway. Every few steps they'd meet a lady they knew. Each boy would remove his round, hard straw hat and bow slightly.

"I want to be polite," said Jimmy, "but it's a lot of trouble. If we go up this alley, we won't meet any ladies."

"I like the Dutch Reformed church," Teddy said, "but it ought to have an alley right beside it. Then we wouldn't have to meet so many people we know."

They turned into the alley and walked along it.

They came to a small puddle of water. Jimmy stopped. He grabbed Teddy by the arm. "See those olive-colored toads with two yellow stripes along their backs."

Teddy stopped and squinted at the puddle. "I

see two toads," he answered. He couldn't see any yellow stripes. He didn't want to admit that the toads just looked gray-black to him.

"I've never seen any like that," said Jimmy. "I bet they're a new kind of toad."

"Then we must have them for the Roosevelt Museum," Teddy said. "You catch one and I'll catch one."

The boys tiptoed on the rough stones. Teddy saw a gray object jump. He pounced on it.

"I've got one, Teddy," yelled Jimmy excitedly.

"I've got one, too," Teddy cried. Now that he held the toad in his hand, he could see the yellow stripes on its back. Underneath, the toad was yellowish-white. He could see the different colors close up, but Jimmy had seen the yellow stripes as soon as he saw the toads.

"What shall we do with them?" Jimmy asked.

Teddy didn't know what to say. He and Jimmy were dressed in their best clothes.

"We can't put them in our pockets," Teddy said. "Mother wouldn't like it, and your mother wouldn't like it either. We'll have to carry them in our hands."

"We'd hurt them," objected Jimmy. "I'm going to be a doctor, and I know."

"All right, Doctor," said Teddy. "Where can we put them?"

The two boys looked at each other. They looked at the toads. The toads flexed their legs and tried to jump from the boys' hands.

Jimmy saw a yellow liquid on his hand. "I've heard that a toad makes warts on you," he said with alarm.

Teddy studied his toad. Then he put his hand up to his head and felt his straw hat. "Say!" His jaws clicked. They always clicked when he spoke excitedly. "We can put them under our hats. You can't have warts on the top of your head, I know."

54

"That's so," Jimmy agreed. He took off his straw hat. "Well, here goes!" He put the toad on his head. Quickly he jerked his hat down. "That works," he announced.

Teddy placed his toad on the top of his head.

He held his hand on it as long as possible. Then he too jerked his hat down. He stood still a moment. "He's there all right." He grinned. "I felt him jump."

The boys started down the alley again. Teddy was thinking hard. "This is a new kind of toad," he said. "I bet nobody has ever seen one like it before. What shall we call it?"

Jimmy stopped to consider the problem. "We both found it. So it has to be named for both of us."

"Come on," said Teddy. "We can think while we walk."

"I can't," objected Jimmy. "Let's see. We can call it *Bufo rooseveltianus*. What do you think about that?"

"What does that mean?" Teddy asked.

"Why, Teddy! *Bufo* is Latin for toad. Papa told me that after I caught a plain one. And we're Roosevelts."

Teddy glared at his cousin. "You mean I have to know Latin to run a museum?"

"Of course, Teddy. All the plants and animals have Latin names. Didn't you know that?"

Teddy did not answer his cousin's question. He was thinking hard. It wasn't enough to call a toad just a toad. There were all kinds of toads.

"Do all kinds of toads have Latin names?" he asked.

"Of course," Jimmy answered. "We couldn't just call it *roosevelt*. First we must say it's a toad. That's *Bufo*. Then we must say what kind of toad it is."

"Could we say just *Bufo roosevelt?* That's part Latin, part Dutch."

"No, we couldn't. It must be all Latin. We'd have to add *rooseveltianus*. That's Latin for Roosevelt."

"Are you sure?" asked Teddy.

"I think so, but I'll ask Papa," said Jimmy.

Teddy frowned. "I guess I'll have to study Latin," he said finally. "Everything in the Roosevelt Museum has to be named right."

At the end of the alley the two boys turned onto a main street. In front of them, people were coming out of the Episcopal church.

Teddy spoke quickly. "Jimmy, we'd better turn back!"

He was too late. Mrs. Hamilton Fish was walking straight toward them.

The two boys drew themselves erect. "Good morning, Mrs. Fish," they said. Each lifted his hat with a flourish.

"Good morning, James. Good morning, Theo——" Mrs. Fish began. She didn't finish the sentence. She screamed and jumped back. Her mouth gaped open in surprise.

But the boys had forgotten her. They looked at each other.

"What happened to your toad?" Teddy asked.

"I don't know," Jimmy answered. "When I raised my hat I felt it hop out."

"So did mine," said Teddy.

Mrs. Fish walked grandly past them, without another word.

They hunted for the toads, but they could not find them.

"They're gone, Teddy," said Jimmy.

"I don't mind for myself," Teddy said bitterly, "but I hate to think of the loss to science. The world will never know of the *Bufo roosevelt-ianus*. Jimmy, just think of the loss to science!"

Fishing for Trout

TEDDY had a bad attack of asthma the summer he was eleven. His mother and father were worried about him.

"I can't get away from New York just now," said Mr. Roosevelt, "but Theodore ought to be out of the city. Let's send him to stay with Brother Rob on Moosehead Lake."

"Rob is so busy writing his book on fishing he couldn't entertain him," Mrs. Roosevelt objected. "Besides, there's no one to take him."

Teddy tried to speak. "Mother, I can go by myself," he finally gasped. "I'm not a baby, even if I do sound like a baby hippopotamus."

Mr. Roosevelt smiled at Teddy's cheerfulness. "Of course he can go alone. Jack's up there with his father. He can keep Theodore company and teach him how to fish."

Two days later Mrs. Roosevelt put Teddy on the train. That part of the trip was wonderful. Then he had to change to a stagecoach. The only vacant place was on the back seat. Two boys, about his age but bigger, were sitting there.

"This is my window," said one boy.

"This one's mine," said the other.

They moved quickly to the outside seats. Teddy took the seat between them. He could see nothing but the sky and the tops of trees through the high windows.

The stagecoach lurched forward. Teddy was thrown to one side.

A sharp elbow punched into his ribs. "Get off me," said the boy on that side. "You're breathing in my ear."

Teddy moved back. He tried to sit very still. His legs were too short to brace solidly against the floor. There were deep ruts in some parts of the road, and soon he was thrown against the same boy again.

"I said stay off me," the boy growled. He gave Teddy a shove toward the other boy.

Teddy tried to sit upright, but his shoulder touched the other boy's. Instantly he was pushed violently away.

"Stop it!" Teddy said. His voice was shaking with anger. He was breathing jerkily again.

"You stop it, kid," the first boy said. He snorted in imitation of Teddy's breathing. The second boy laughed. Then he too wheezed.

For several minutes the two boys wheezed and snorted and laughed. Teddy blushed and doubled up his fists, but he sat still.

Then the coach hit another rough spot. The three boys rocked against one another.

"I said hold still," said the boy on the right.

"Let's make him stay put, Tony," said the other. He grabbed Teddy's left arm with both hands. Tony's hands clutched Teddy's right arm and shoulder.

Teddy squirmed in his seat and tried to pull his arms free. Tony's fingers were long and hard. They pinched.

Teddy struggled as hard as he could for a few minutes, but he couldn't free his arms and he couldn't use his fists. He tried to butt with his head or to kick. That was no good either.

The coach rumbled across a bridge. Tony looked out the window. "Say, we're almost home," he said.

A few minutes later the coach stopped at a small town. Giving Teddy a final shove the two boys climbed out.

"Good-by, Old Wheezer," they called to him as they jumped down.

Teddy stared at the boys as they ran across the square. He was angrier than he had ever been in his life, but he was most angry at himself. He had never thought that anyone might try to push him around like that. "It's never going to happen to me again," he told himself. He felt his arm muscles. "I'm going to have good muscles, and I'm going to learn how to use them."

TEDDY CAN'T FISH

The next morning Teddy and Jack went fishing. They walked down to the little dock. They put their fishing rods and other tackle in the birchbark canoe. Then each of them got a paddle.

"The fish are biting over near the west bank," Jack said as he pushed the canoe away from the dock.

Teddy enjoyed paddling. He liked to feel the paddle cut through the water.

"You make too much noise when you paddle," Jack protested.

"I like to go fast," replied Teddy.

"I like to go quietly. You scare the fish away with all that noise," said Jack disgustedly.

"They can't hear us," retorted Teddy. "Besides, we're not ready to fish."

"They *can* hear us, Teddy," answered Jack. "We're almost there. Now, don't talk anymore."

Teddy tried to paddle silently. The canoe slowed down.

Jack liked to fish. He looked over his rod and line carefully. He looked to see if his brightly colored fly was just right. Then he lifted his right arm. He held the pole firmly. Then he cast by quickly flipping the pole and releasing the line. It spun out with a whirring sound. Yet the fly hit the water gently.

Teddy was impatient. He lifted the pole above his head. He threw the line out. The fly smacked the water.

"Take it easy," Jack whispered. He began to reel in his line.

For an hour they caught nothing. Then Jack said tensely, "I've got one." He began to play the fish carefully. He let it run a little way in the water. Then he started to pull it in. At last he said, "Hand me that net, Teddy."

Teddy laid his pole in the bottom of the canoe. Then he reached down and got the net. He passed it to Jack.

"There," said Jack. "I've got him!"

Teddy looked at the speckled trout flopping in the net. "That's a beauty."

"Won't weigh over a pound," Jack said. "I thought he was bigger." He dropped the fish into a wet sack in the canoe.

Teddy cast a good many times. Finally he felt

a quick tug on the line. He began to reel in the line fast. Suddenly it went slack.

"You didn't let him really bite the hook," said Jack. "You should let him run a little."

Teddy nodded. He was not satisfied with himself. He couldn't fight. He couldn't fish. Sometimes he couldn't even breathe without making a wheezing noise.

Right now he must learn to fish. He watched Jack closely. His cousin had a smooth, easy swing. It let the fly settle on the water. Teddy knew that his own fly just dropped on the water.

He practiced hard. Once he got a small trout on his hook. This time he let it run a little before he began to pull it in.

Jack had the net ready. "Here, Teddy."

Teddy scooped the net under the fish. The shining, speckled trout leaped up, but it couldn't get out of the net. "Gee, it's a beauty!" Teddy cried in excitement.

Three days later Teddy and Jack again paddled across the lake. Now Teddy dipped his paddle smoothly into the water. The canoe made no noise.

"I'm not breathing like a hippopotamus any longer," Teddy thought, "and I can paddle almost as silently as Jack."

They let the canoe slow down.

Theodore looked carefully at his pole and line. He made sure that the fly was on tight. He cast smoothly. Slowly he pulled the fly through the water.

He felt a fish strike hard at the hook. "Say, I've got a big one," he said excitedly. He let the fish run a little. Then he started to pull it in. The fish fought hard. The pole bent. Teddy let it run a little more.

He began to play the fish. He pulled it in a little. The fish plunged. Teddy loosened the

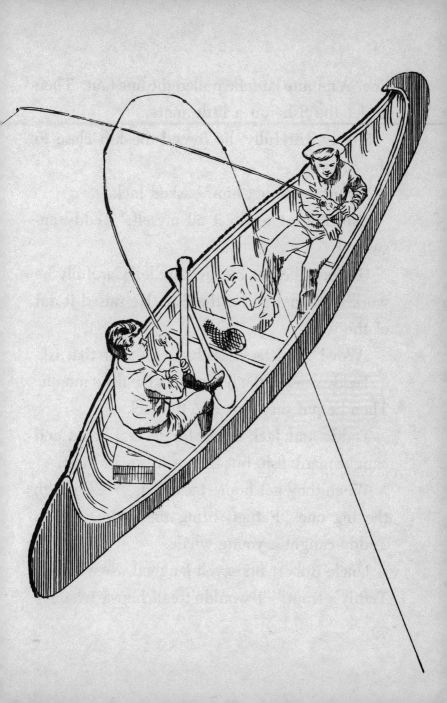

line. A minute later he pulled the line taut. Then he let the fish run a little more.

Slowly, carefully, he forced the fish close to the canoe.

"Want me to net him?" asked Jack.

"No, I want to do it all myself," Teddy answered.

He took the net by the handle. Carefully he worked the net under the fish. He raised it out of the water.

"Wow!" said Jack. "What a wonder that is!"

Teddy worked the hook out of the fish's mouth. Then he put the trout into the sack.

Teddy and Jack fished for several hours and caught many fish, but they were small trout.

When they got home Jack said, "We'll weigh the big one. Father, bring the scales, please. Teddy caught a young whale."

Uncle Robert Roosevelt laughed when he saw Teddy's trout. "I wouldn't call him a whale—

not even a baby whale. But he's worth weighing." He put the trout on the scales. "Two pounds exactly. Why, it weighs as much as the one you caught, Jack. He can't crow over you now, Teddy."

Teddy was frowning.

Mr. Roosevelt looked at his nephew with surprise. "You're not jealous because it isn't bigger, are you?"

Teddy forced a smile. "No, sir. Jack's a better fisherman than I ever will be. I was thinking of something else."

He liked fishing and he liked Jack. He hoped Jack would catch a three-pound trout. He was frowning because he remembered how the two boys on the stagecoach had pushed him around. They had really crowed over him. He hadn't been able to protect himself. He must make his body strong. He would talk to his father about that as soon as he got back to New York.

A Mouse and a Gymnasium

A MONTH later, on a warm September afternoon, Teddy got home from Moosehead Lake. The maid, Dora, opened the door for him. "How're you feeling, Master Theodore?" she asked. "Did you have a nice trip?"

"Just fine," Teddy answered. Something was wrong about the house. There wasn't a sound to be heard. "What makes everything so quiet?"

"There's nobody home but your father," said Dora, smiling. "He's upstairs in his study. Your mother and Miss Anna and the children have all gone to your grandfather's. You'd better hurry up. Maybe you can go, too."

Teddy nodded. It was fun to go to his grandfather Roosevelt's house. He could slide down the great, curving staircase. But first he wanted to talk with his father.

He went upstairs and knocked on the study door. "Come in," Mr. Roosevelt called in his deep voice. "Theodore! I'm glad to see you."

He shook Theodore's hand warmly. "You're looking a whole lot better, son. But we can talk later. Run along and change clothes. We haven't much time before dinner at your grandfather's."

Teddy held himself erect. "Father, I want to talk with you first." His voice was firm, but he had to fight with himself to hold it steady.

"Is it important?" Mr. Roosevelt asked.

"Yes, sir."

"Then sit down, and let's have it."

"I can think better when I'm walking." Teddy began to pace up and down. There wasn't any easy way to say it, although he had planned his speech carefully. His jaws clicked as he started to speak. "On the stagecoach going up to the lake there were two boys. They were about my age, but they were bigger. I sat between them. I—I don't think they were bad boys." He stopped.

"Yes, Theodore. Go on. What happened?" Mr. Roosevelt's voice was kind. He was listening carefully to every word his son said.

"They held me. They pushed me back and forth." Teddy's tone was still bitter as he ended. "Papa, they handled me just like a baby," he blurted out. "I don't want that ever to happen to me again."

"Come here, Theodore. Let me take a good look at you."

The boy walked over and stood in front of his father.

"You've been sick with asthma nearly all your life, son," Mr. Roosevelt said finally. "Your

76

chest is narrow. You have small arms and small legs. You have never been able to run and play as hard as most boys your age, but you find so much to keep you busy I haven't worried."

"But, Papa, I don't want to stay sick all my life. I want to be strong."

Mr. Roosevelt stood up. He put his hands on his son's shoulders. "You've grown taller this summer," he said. "It's time we did something about those muscles." He shook his head gravely. "But you can't build strong muscles in a few weeks. You can't even do it in a few months."

"I'll work hard at it," Teddy promised. "I want this more than I ever wanted anything in my life."

"Let me think about it," said Mr. Roosevelt. "Now, go bathe quickly. And do comb your hair. It looks like a mop."

"I like to wear it *à la mop*," said Teddy, grinning and shaking his head.

"Well, I don't like it. There was just one man in history who had great strength because he wore long hair. That was Samson, in the Bible. But it was several thousand years ago."

Teddy ran his hand through his hair. "I'd like to be stronger than Samson."

"Well, you won't be. He was the strongest man that ever lived. But you can be as strong as most boys. You'll have to exercise your muscles. There isn't any easy way, like letting your hair grow long."

"I know there isn't," said Teddy. "I'll get a haircut tomorrow, I promise."

A HUNT IN THE PARK

The next afternoon a delivery wagon drawn by two stout horses stopped in front of the Roosevelt house. A man got out and knocked at the door. The maid opened it. "Is this Mr. Theodore Roosevelt's house?" he asked.

"Yes," Dora answered.

"I have a lot of stuff that goes here," the man said. "Where do you want it?"

"I don't know," answered Dora. "I'll ask Mrs. Roosevelt."

Theodore, Elliott, and Corinne were looking out the window.

"I wonder what we're getting, Teedie?" said Conie eagerly.

Mrs. Roosevelt came to the door. The children crowded close to her. They were looking at the wagon.

"Dora!" Mrs. Roosevelt called. "Take the children to the park. They'd be right underfoot here all the time. One of them is sure to get hurt."

"But we want to stay and see the new things," Teddy objected.

Elliott and Corinne wanted to do whatever Theodore was doing. So Mrs. Roosevelt suggested, "Maybe you can catch that mouse Theodore's been wanting."

"If I catch it, may I keep it?" Teddy asked.

"Yes," his mother answered. "But don't ask Dora to touch it. You know she's afraid of mice."

"I'm not," said Conie. "I'll help you, Teedie."

She ran off, calling loudly, "Dora! Let's go. We're going to catch a mouse."

When he was sure that Conie couldn't see him, Teddy made a face and grinned at his mother. "You know she gets in my way. But I'll catch one in spite of her help," he said.

A NEW SPECIMEN FOR THE MUSEUM

At the park the three children searched for field mice. They turned over rocks. They looked into holes in trees and under roots and piles of leaves.

"There's one," said Conie. "I saw it." She pointed with a finger.

Teddy watched. He saw something gray. It darted across the path in front of him. "That must be a squirrel," he said. "We can't catch a squirrel. It moves too fast."

Conie and Ellie got tired of looking. They went off to wade in the pool. Teddy kept on searching.

A man was watching him. "What are you looking for, boy?" he asked.

Teddy looked up. "A mouse," he said. "I need it for my museum."

"What museum is that?"

"The Roosevelt Museum of Natural History. I have two white mice. I need a brown mouse."

"I have a warehouse near here. We have all kinds of mice. We have more mice than we

know what to do with. Want to try your luck there?"

Teddy liked the looks of the man. But he hesitated. "I can't, sir. Maybe if I told Dora——"

"We'll tell Dora where you're going." The man went over and talked with Dora.

"It's all right, Master Theodore," the maid called to him. "I've known Mr. Daley all my life."

Teddy and Mr. Daley walked along the city street. "I bought the white mice," Teddy said. "But I want to catch the brown one myself."

"That won't be easy," Mr. Daley said. "Do you have a cage?"

"No, I thought I'd slip up on a mouse."

"You won't be able to do that. There's a cage at the warehouse. It isn't a trap that kills a mouse or rat. We'll need some cheese for bait."

They stopped at a store. Mr. Daley bought some yellow cheese.

They came to the warehouse. Mr. Daley opened the door. It was dark inside.

"I'll go to the office and get the cage," Mr. Daley said. "You wait here."

In a minute he returned with the cage. "This is a grain warehouse," he said. "There are always rats and mice here. But they're timid. They may not come out until night."

The warehouse didn't seem so dark now. Mr. Daley put the bait in the cage.

"May I watch it?" said Teddy.

"If you make even the slightest sound, you'll scare the mice off."

"I won't make a sound," Teddy promised.

"Then get up on those bales of hay," said Mr. Daley. He set the cage near a corner. "If you catch a mouse, come up front to the office. I'll be working there."

Teddy climbed up on the hay. He stretched out so that he could watch the cage.

He lay there for what seemed like hours. The hay scratched his knees and arms. He wanted to move, but he didn't dare to move much. He wanted to sneeze. With a finger he pressed hard against his upper lip.

Something moved. Teddy watched intently. A gray-brown shape was sneaking toward the cage.

"It's too big to be a mouse. It must be a rat. I'll take it home anyway," Teddy thought. "But Mother won't like it a bit."

The gray-brown rat sniffed at the cage. Then it walked around it.

Teddy was tense. He was straining to see every movement of the rat, but the rat crept away from the cage. It disappeared in the shadows.

Teddy settled back to wait some more. The sharp, dry hay made his skin itch.

After a long time he heard light pattering sounds. He heard something squeal. But the warehouse had grown darker. He couldn't see a thing where the sound came from.

He continued watching. Once he saw a quick-moving shadow. A moment later he heard a faint squealing near the cage.

Again the warehouse was silent. Teddy couldn't see anything or hear anything.

He heard someone moving in the front of the building. Suddenly he sneezed loudly: *"Ker-choo-ow! Ker-choo!"*

Mr. Daley called, "Did you get one?"

"I don't know," answered Teddy. "I couldn't see whether the mouse went in the cage or not." He climbed down from the hay.

Mr. Daley joined him. "If it didn't, you'll have to come back in the morning. I have a wagon at the back that must be unloaded. The noise will scare every mouse into its hole."

Teddy lifted the cage. A small brown mouse dashed against the wire.

"We caught one!" he said excitedly. "I have a mouse for my museum."

"Take it home in the cage. You can bring the cage back tomorrow."

"I had fun watching the cage," said Teddy. "But it's a lot harder work doing nothing than it is doing something."

He hurried toward the park. The afternoon light was fading.

Teddy couldn't find Dora or Ellie or Conie. He was disappointed. He wanted to show them his brown mouse.

THE PUNCHING BAG

Teddy ran home. The cage was swinging in his hand.

Mr. Roosevelt opened the door. "Come with me, Theodore. I've something to show you."

"I caught a brown mouse, Father," he said excitedly and held up the cage.

"That's good," said Mr. Roosevelt. He too seemed excited. Teddy thought it was about the mouse. "Come upstairs, son. I've something better than a mouse to show you."

Teddy was disappointed. His father wasn't interested in the mouse. He followed slowly up the stairs.

The Roosevelt house had three stories. The

house was narrow with houses joined to it on each side. On the second floor there was a back porch. The porch had a strong, high railing around it and a roof over it.

Mr. Roosevelt threw open the door. "Look at that," he said.

Teddy looked. "A punching bag!" he exclaimed. He darted about the porch. "Whee! A seesaw! And parallel bars! Golly, Papa, is this all for me?"

Mr. Roosevelt smiled. "Well, mainly it is, Theodore. But all of you children will have fun using it."

"Hurray! Now I can get strong. Oh, Papa, thank you so much!"

"It won't be easy, son. You have a good mind, but you must have a strong body, too. You'll have to build your strength yourself. It will be dull, hard work, but you can do it."

"I *can* do it," said Theodore with determination. "And I will, too. You don't know how much I thank you, Papa."

"Just use this gymnasium every day," said Mr. Roosevelt. "That's all I ask."

Elliott came through the door. "Oh, Ellie," Teddy cried, "hasn't this been a wonderful day? I caught a brown mouse for my museum. And now we have a gymnasium."

The Shotgun

"Wake up, Teddy! It's Christmas," said Elliott.

"I'm awake. I was thinking. I'll bet we have the best Christmases in the world." Teddy wiggled his toes. The bed was warm and pleasant.

Elliott began to fidget. "I'll bet I get a red express wagon. And heaps of candy."

Teddy looked out the window. "I can see light in the sky. It *is* time to get up." He jumped out of bed. The room was cold. Teddy dressed quickly, before he washed his face and hands.

Corinne pushed the door open. "Hurry up, slowpokes!" she yelled at her brothers. "I can't wait any longer."

"Christmas gift, Conie!" shouted Teddy. "I was the first one to say it."

"Come on," Conie said impatiently.

She hurried down the hall. The boys followed her. She threw open the door to their parents' bedroom.

"Christmas gift," shouted Teddy, "to Mother and Father!"

"Merry Christmas to all," said Mr. and Mrs. Roosevelt together.

"I caught everybody in saying it," said Teddy happily. "Now all of you owe me Christmas gifts."

"You haven't caught Bamie," said Elliott. "She isn't here."

"You needn't wait for her," Mrs. Roosevelt told them. "Get your stockings and crawl up on the bed."

"My, they look nice and bulky!" said Teddy. He took his stocking from the mantel and climbed up on the bed. He began to pull the presents out of the stocking. "A banana. A compass. Goody! And a pocketknife with a long blade."

Teddy stopped to examine the knife. "That's just what I wanted," he said. He looked up. His oldest sister was just coming into the room. "Christmas gift, Bamie! Now I guess I've caught everybody."

When each one had emptied a stocking, Mrs. Roosevelt said, "Now let's go downstairs. We'll have breakfast immediately."

"Can't we just peek into the library?" Conie begged.

"No," said Mrs. Roosevelt. "Not until we've had prayers and breakfast."

When breakfast was at last over, Mr. Roosevelt opened the door to the library. "Corinne's the smallest. She gets to go first. Then Elliott. Then Theodore."

"I won't make you wait," Conie said. She scampered into the library.

Teddy saw the four tables, one for each child. At the very first glance he knew which table was his.

"That's my shotgun!" he shouted. He lifted the gun carefully, lovingly, from the table. He dashed to his father. "That's just exactly what I wanted," he said gratefully.

Mr. Roosevelt dodged away from the gun. "Be careful, Theodore." He laughed. "You know how to handle a gun better than that. You're supposed to shoot game with it, not us. Are you surprised?"

"You bet I am!" Teddy turned to Mrs. Roosevelt. "Thanks, Mother. You said I couldn't have a gun until I was fourteen. I was only twelve last October."

"Just be careful," said his mother. "You are very young to have a gun."

"When can I go hunting?" asked Teddy.

"We're going out to your grandfather's house at Oyster Bay this morning," Mr. Roosevelt said. "You can take your gun along. I'll show you how to use it."

"I MUST HAVE GLASSES"

It was three o'clock before the Christmas dinner was finished. The dining room was crowded. Grandfather Cornelius Van Shaak Roosevelt, who was now old and feeble, had invited his five sons and their families. There were twenty-one Roosevelts at the table.

Teddy sat between his cousins Jimmy and Jack. They were his partners in the Roosevelt Museum. They too had received new shotguns for Christmas. The three boys had hunted with their fathers, but they'd used small rifles before.

When the last person had finished the plum

pudding, Teddy said, "Grandfather, may we be excused? Jimmy and Jack and I want to go hunting."

Old Mr. Roosevelt looked at his five grown sons. "I think we can get through the afternoon without these boys, don't you?" His eyes twinkled. "Just don't shoot one another, boys."

The boys walked very quietly out of the dining room. Then they scampered down the hall to get their shotguns.

"What shall we hunt?" asked Teddy.

"Rabbits," Jack suggested.

"There's not much snow," objected Jimmy. "We couldn't find their tracks."

"We need some squirrels for the museum," Teddy said. "I know how to skin them and stuff them now. Mr. Bell, the man who stuffs animals, taught me how to do it."

"He taught me, too," Jimmy said. "We can keep the stuffed animals for years."

"I'll just kill the game for you," said Jack. "I don't like to cut it up. That's a messy job."

"You'll never be a scientist," Teddy said. He loaded both barrels of his gun.

"I don't want to be, Teddy," retorted Jack. "I'm going to be a lawyer."

The boys walked along the sandy shore of the bay. The wind was cold on their cheeks. It made little whitecaps in the water.

They came to the edge of the woods. Suddenly Jimmy stopped them. He aimed his gun at a tree some distance away.

"I don't see anything," said Teddy. He could see the tree, but he couldn't locate anything in it.

Jimmy sighted along the barrel. He pulled the trigger. The gun roared. "Missed him," said Jimmy disgustedly. He rubbed his right shoulder. "Say, this thing kicks."

"What were you shooting at?" Teddy asked.

"Just a sparrow," his cousin answered.

"Let's scatter out and shoot at everything we see," suggested Jack. "We must learn how to use these guns."

"Let's shoot only at things in trees," said Teddy. "We might hit one another if we shot at a rabbit."

"That's right," Jimmy agreed. "Let's go. We'll meet at the road."

They separated, and Teddy started walking through the woods. He held his gun ready. He looked hard at the trees.

To his left a gun roared. A few minutes later he heard another gun roar.

"I haven't seen a thing yet," he thought.

He walked on as quietly as he could. There! In a pine tree he saw something dark. It seemed to move.

Teddy lifted the gun. It was hard to hold it straight on the target. He sighted carefully and pulled the trigger.

The noise hurt his ears. The gun seemed to throw him backward. There was a pain in his right shoulder. "Jimmy was right. It sure does kick," he said to himself.

Something brown had fallen out of the tree.

Teddy hurried to find it. There was no squirrel under the tree, but he found two pine cones.

"So that's what I shot at," he thought. "But maybe it wasn't. Maybe there was a squirrel on the limb. I'm not sure."

Teddy heard more shots, but he couldn't see anything to shoot at. It was getting dark in the woods. He walked on hopelessly.

Jimmy was waiting at the road. "What did you get? I got two squirrels."

"I didn't get a thing," Teddy admitted.

Jimmy pointed down the road. "We could go shoot at the pigeons on that barn roof."

Teddy looked. "I can't see them. What's that red and black stuff on the side?"

"Why, Teddy!" Jimmy looked at his cousin in amazement. "That's an advertisement. The red is a picture of a pound of coffee, and the black says in big letters, ARBUCKLE'S COFFEE. Can't you read that?"

Teddy couldn't. Even now that he'd been told what the letters were, he couldn't make them out. They were only a dark blur in the distance. He could see some red and he could see some black, but that was all.

Jack came out of the woods. "I got a squirrel," he said proudly. "Knocked him right off a limb."

"We'd better get home," said Jimmy quickly. "We're going back to New York tonight. It's almost an hour by the train."

Jimmy didn't say what he'd shot, or that Teddy had failed to shoot anything. Teddy knew that Jimmy was trying to help him.

"Thanks, Jimmy," Teddy said warmly. He turned to Jack and admitted, "I didn't hit anything. I didn't see a bird or an animal. At least, I didn't know it if I did."

"That's all right, Teddy," said Jack. "You'll do better next time."

"No, I won't," Teddy said. "I know what's

the matter with me. I must have glasses. I'll hate to wear them, but I hate worse not seeing a sign as big as a barn door. Someday I'm going to hunt big game for our museum, and I'll have to live in the woods. I want to shoot my supper and cook it myself, but I can't shoot anything when I can't see it."

Young Mr. Four-Eyes

ONE AFTERNOON in January, Teddy walked home wearing his new glasses. He read every sign above the stores. The lines of the buildings were clear and distinct. The bricks and stones looked much brighter.

He took off his glasses. The red bricks looked paler, the buildings darker.

He put them on again. His own brownstone house seemed cleaner and prettier than ever. He stopped suddenly to look more closely at it.

Someone bumped into him from behind. He turned around. "Keep moving," said a little boy angrily. "You stopped right in front of me."

The youngster doubled his right fist. "Out of my way," he ordered, "or I'll knock you out!" He looked up at Teddy. "Hey, Four-eyes! What you wearing those for? Only old folks wear glasses."

Teddy's grin showed his strong white teeth. "I can see better with them on," he said. "That's a mighty good reason."

The boy undoubled his fist. "I can't hit a kid who wears glasses," he said. He darted around Teddy and ran up the street.

Mrs. Roosevelt opened the door. "Come on in, Theodore. You've been gone so long I was getting anxious." She looked at her son. "Your glasses look very nice on you. Do they fit all right?"

"They feel funny," Teddy answered, "but they're just wonderful. Oh, Mother, it's like living in a new world!"

"Don't strain your eyes. Read as much as you

like, but quit whenever your eyes get tired." His mother's voice was sympathetic. "It may take a few days to get used to your glasses."

"I'm used to them now. Mother, a funny thing happened. Some boy ran into me and wanted to fight. When he saw my glasses he called me Four-eyes. I don't like it."

"You'll have to get used to that, too, son. Many people make fun of physical weaknesses. It's unkind, but they do."

"I'm not going to be weak. I can chin myself ten times without stopping." Teddy added thoughtfully, "I don't think the boy meant to be mean. When he saw my glasses, he quit wanting to fight."

"He was just thoughtless," said Mrs. Roosevelt. "I don't want you fighting, Theodore."

"Mother, I'd better go skip the rope and punch on my bag. Then I'll study. I don't want to fight. But if I must, I want to be ready."

106

Every Sunday evening Teddy went with his father to the Newsboys' Lodginghouse. He liked the boys, and he liked the free and easy way they treated him. He could see that many of them were hungry and dirty most of the time. They were boys after his own heart, and he was eager to do whatever he could for them.

"Father," he said thoughtfully one evening, "I'm worried about my friend Mike the newsboy. He has a bad cough."

Mr. Roosevelt nodded. "I've noticed it," he said, "and I've written a friend of mine out in South Dakota. He has a cattle ranch. I think we'd better send Mike out there."

Teddy nodded. "I'll hate not seeing Mike. But when I grow up, maybe I can go out and hunt with him. Can I tell him tonight?"

"Why, of course," Mr. Roosevelt replied.

To Teddy's surprise, Mike was not certain

that he wanted to go out west. "I know the ropes here, Teddy," he said, "but I don't know which end of a cow to milk."

"This is a cattle ranch," Teddy answered. "You don't milk the cows. You ride a horse and rope cows."

"Oh!" said Mike. "I'd like that."

"So would I," said Teddy.

A week later Teddy said good-by to Mike. "I'll keep going to those Newsboys' dinners, but it'll never be the same again," he told his friend.

LIKE WASHINGTON AND LINCOLN

Teddy had always been taught at home in the room next to the gymnasium. His Aunt Anna had married now, so there were no more stories of Br'er Rabbit.

A young Frenchwoman taught him French one hour a day. She always motioned with her hands when she talked. Teddy liked her, but he could never pronounce the French words to please her.

A Mr. Robinson taught him English, Latin, arithmetic, and history. He had just finished reading a theme that Teddy had written on George Washington. "How do you spell *general?*" Mr. Robinson asked.

Teddy hesitated. "G-e-n—" He stopped, then added quickly, "r-a-l."

"At least you spelled it the same way you did in the theme. But you were wrong both times. Try it again."

Teddy tried to remember how the word looked in the history book. "G-e-n-e-r-a-l."

"That's right. You read so fast you barely see the words. I hope your glasses are helping you."

"Spelling's too hard," Teddy said. "I could make it a lot easier. History and natural science are easy."

"They are for you because you like them," said Mr. Robinson. "So you think Washington was the greatest American?"

"Yes, sir, he was!" Teddy leaned forward and spoke earnestly. "He was a great general, and then he was our first President. 'First in war, first in peace, and first in the hearts of his countrymen!' That's what our history book says he was called."

"What does that mean, Teddy?"

"It means that all Americans knew they could depend on him. In war he was the general, and the soldiers knew they could depend on him. After the war the people made him President, because they knew they could depend on him, too. And everybody loved him."

Teddy jumped up. His eyes were shining. "I like that picture of him in the boat crossing the Delaware River. He was standing up like this." Teddy took a pose with his head thrown back and his shoulders straight. "The men knew he was the leader. It was cold, and the men were ragged, and there weren't many of them. But he wasn't afraid, and so they weren't afraid either. It's a bully picture!"

"Do you boys play soldiers?" Mr. Robinson asked quietly.

"Yes, sir. We like to play soldiers." Teddy hesitated a moment. "I'd like to play President, too, but I don't know how we'd do that."

"Your father might tell you how," Mr. Robinson suggested. "He was a good friend of Abraham Lincoln, and of Mrs. Lincoln, too."

"Father talks about President Lincoln sometimes," Teddy agreed. "About how the President wanted the government to protect every honest citizen. Father says that President Lincoln believed that the government ought to be of the people, by the people, and for the people."

Mr. Robinson nodded. "Do you believe that, too, Teddy?"

"Yes, sir," the boy answered without hesitation. He spoke with strong feeling. "A general should look after his soldiers. That's what Washington did. And a President should look after the people. Washington did that. And Lincoln did, too. He wanted every man to be free and independent. A general is important when there's a war, but a President is important all the time to his country."

Teddy sat down. He thought a minute and then looked at his teacher. "It would be fun to be President," he confided. "When I grow up I'm going to work to help make this country strong, just as Washington and Lincoln did."

Capturing the Fort

THE FAMILY spent that summer at Oyster Bay. One August morning Mr. Roosevelt said to his eldest son, "Theodore, I want to talk with you before you go play. Are you in a hurry?"

"I promised Dave Lloyd yesterday I'd row over and play with him. But I didn't tell him when I'd get there."

"Then come into the library for a few moments." When they were inside the room Mr. Roosevelt said, "You're looking a great deal better, Theodore. Your mother and I are very much pleased about it."

Teddy felt proudly of his muscles. "I go horseback riding every morning before breakfast. I row a boat or go swimming every pretty afternoon. When it rains I punch the bag hard."

"I hope you're completely over being sick. In fact, I hope you're well enough to go to school in September. Would you like that?"

"You bet I would! I'd like it better than almost anything," Teddy answered excitedly.

Mr. Roosevelt smiled. "Studying by yourself, or just with Elliott, isn't much fun, is it? Well, Mr. Robinson has written that he'd like to go back to Harvard this fall. I'll write to Professor McMullen, back home in New York, about you and Elliott right away. Jack went to his academy last year, and Rob was pleased with the school."

COLONEL TEDDY

One day in September, when he was almost thirteen years old, Teddy went to school for the first time. Professor McMullen's Academy, on Twentieth Street, was close enough for him to live at home and walk to school each day with his brother Elliott and his cousin Jack.

Teddy liked all the boys at the academy. "I missed a lot, studying at home," he thought.

School was fun. Teddy had always enjoyed reading. Now he enjoyed competing with the other boys to answer the questions asked by the teachers. He knew more history than anyone else in his grade. He knew French and a little Latin, and he knew about birds and animals.

On sunny days, though, he could hardly wait for school to let out. Every clear afternoon the boys played soldiers.

An old stable at one corner of the schoolyard served as a fort. One afternoon the Blue army would defend it, and the Gray army would try to capture it. The next afternoon the Gray army would try to hold the fort.

Teddy belonged to the Blue Army. A boy named Fred Osborn was their general.

"We've got to capture that fort today, Teddy," said Fred. "We've failed three times. If we fail again, the boys will elect a new general."

"But they didn't capture us, either, when we were defending," Teddy reminded him.

There were eighteen boys on each side. Each boy had a wooden sword. When the attacking army got ten boys inside, it had captured the fort. Neither side had been able to do it. Mr. Mcmullen had ruled that when a boy was touched by an enemy's sword, that boy was "dead." He wouldn't allow any of the boys to get hurt.

"I'm going to send Jack with five men to attack the side windows," said Fred. "The rest of us will attack the big door at the front."

"We did that day before yesterday," Teddy objected. "It didn't work."

The Blue army was waiting. The Gray army

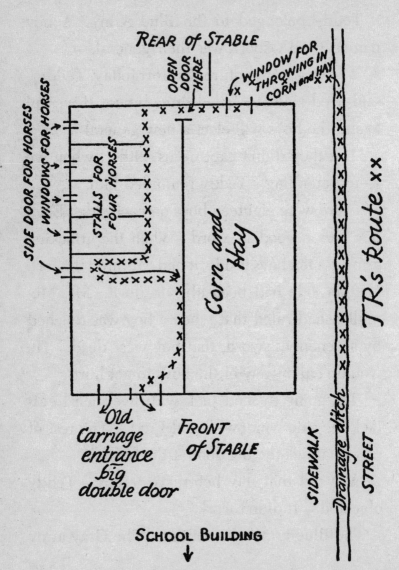

Map of the fort and Teddy's route.

was in the fort. The defenders would give the signal when war was to begin.

"Fred doesn't know what to do," said one boy scornfully.

"I'll bet I could do better," said a second boy.

"What would you do?"

"I'd burst right through that door."

"You and who else?" asked a third boy.

Teddy was looking hard at the stable and at the yard. He looked at the shallow ditch at the edge of the street. "Say, Fred! I've sneaked up on animals. I'll bet I could crawl back along that ditch without the enemy ever seeing me. So could Jack and Ellie."

Fred examined the ditch. "What would you do if you got to the back of the fort?"

"I'd get inside. That back window won't lock. We know it, and I'll bet they don't."

"It's higher than your head," Fred objected.

"I can chin myself twenty times," Teddy retorted. "Jack can give me a boost. Then I'll open that side door and let you in."

"They'll kill you." Fred was partly convinced. He couldn't think of any other plan that might succeed.

"They won't kill me before I get the door open," Teddy answered stoutly.

The boys in the fort were taking a long time to get ready. General Fred Osborn was now anxious to fight. "Soldiers! Attention!" He spoke in a commanding voice. "Colonel Hill, take those five soldiers nearest you. Attack the big door. Make them think you are going to charge it."

"But we can't," protested the young colonel.

"Make them think you can. You, Captain Teddy Roosevelt—you're captain today. Take Jack and Ellie Roosevelt. You know what to do. The rest of you follow me when I give the word."

Someone inside the stable beat on a drum.

The war was on.

Captain Teddy Roosevelt dropped to the ground. He crawled to the ditch and dropped into it.

He felt cold water soaking through his clothes. But this was war. He crawled through moist, smelly mud.

"Say! I don't like this," Ellie said loudly.

Captain Roosevelt turned his head. "Keep quiet, Private Roosevelt," he commanded sternly. Elliott was his younger brother. He'd have to obey. But Teddy wasn't so certain of Jack. "You, Lieutenant Roosevelt—guard the rear!"

Jack chuckled. "Thanks for the promotion, Teddy. I can eat as much mud as you can."

It was slow, hard work. Teddy felt stones cut into his knees. His shoulders began to ache. But he kept on.

No one was paying attention to them. He crawled along parallel with the stable. He waited a moment, expecting the defenders to shout at him. All that he heard was noise from the front of the building.

"Keep going," Ellie muttered. "I'm cold."

Teddy crawled carefully on. At the back of the fort he'd have to stand upright and run toward the window. He stopped there a moment to get his breath.

"Follow me!" Captain Teddy Roosevelt whispered. He got up. No one had seen them yet. Bent over, he dashed toward the fort.

He was under the window.

Jack and Ellie lifted him up. Teddy grasped the window sill. With the same motion he used to chin himself, Teddy slowly drew himself up.

He was in the window. No one shouted at him.

Quickly he dropped to the floor. He crawled along the back wall and through the open door in the partition between the storage room and the stalls.

He couldn't get near the side door or windows. The Gray army was defending them. Teddy crawled along the side of the room away from the back wall. When he got to the dark corner he pulled out his sword. With all his might he hurled the sword against the back wall.

Ellie's face appeared at the window. "What in thunder!" he yelled.

The whole Gray army dashed toward the back of the stable.

Captain Teddy slipped around them. Not a Gray soldier saw him. He opened the side door.

"Storm the fort!" General Osborn shouted.

The general and eight of the Blue army crowded hastily through the small door. But Teddy had gone on. He opened the big door, too. "This way, Colonel Hill!"

Six more Blue soldiers invaded the fort.

"Boys," yelled General Osborn, "we really whipped them that time! And not a man lost."

"I expect they killed Ellie," said Teddy sadly, "and maybe Jack."

Ellie lifted himself through the window. "I'm not killed," he announced indignantly. "Jack couldn't hold me up. I fell like a ton of bricks. It didn't feel a bit good when I hit the ground."

The Gray army surrendered.

"We win," said General Osborn. "Captain Roosevelt, step forward."

Teddy moved in front of the soldiers.

General Osborn looked at him gratefully. "You're not Captain Roosevelt any longer. From now on, you're Colonel Teddy Roosevelt."

Young
Naturalist

THE ENTIRE Roosevelt family was in Egypt for the winter of 1872–73.

They had gone from New York to England, to visit with Mrs. Roosevelt's brothers. Theodore and Elliott had enjoyed England.

But Teddy liked Egypt better. "It's the land of my dreams, Conie," he told his youngest sister. "And here I can go hunting."

The Roosevelts had rented a houseboat. They were going up the Nile River.

The children were in the cabin shared by Theodore and Elliott.

"I like living on a houseboat," Teddy said.

"It's fun to go to sleep with the river going past, and the boat standing still. But we're going mighty slow now."

"The boat seems to be moving all the time— even when it's tied to the bank," said Conie. "I don't like it, Teddy." Even Conie called him Teddy now.

"You know it isn't, Conie. That's all that matters." Teddy was searching through his suitcase. "I'm glad we've left the cities. I like being out in the country better." He continued to search.

"I enjoyed seeing the Pyramids," said Conie. "Just imagine, all those big stones going 'way up into the air! Like a triangle in a book, only the Pyramids rise up out of the sand."

"I like the Sphinx better," Ellie said. "Its stone nose is bigger than a big man."

"An Egyptian had to pull you up the Pyramids, and another one had to push you," said Teddy. "I wouldn't let one push me, but I'm older than

127

you are. I'm already fourteen, and you aren't quite thirteen."

"It was as scary as climbing straight up a mountain," Elliott defended himself. "Let's go see how fast we're going."

"Wait a minute." Teddy continued to hunt through his suitcase. "I know they're here."

"What, Teddy?" asked his sister.

"My Roosevelt Museum labels, Conie. Every time I kill a strange bird I write down its name and all about it."

"Oh, those things!" said Conie. "I don't see why you want to kill the poor pretty birds."

"Of course I don't like to kill them. I'd much rather catch them. But I can't take them home alive—you know that. People back home should have a chance to see what they really look like in life."

"I never thought of that," Conie said slowly. "I guess your way is best—stuffing and mounting them."

"Yes, it's for science," said Teddy. "Whoops! Here they are." He pulled out a pack of paper labels. On each one, in pink ink, was printed in capital letters: THE ROOSEVELT MUSEUM OF NATURAL HISTORY. "Jimmy and Jack printed these for me. I must get busy."

The houseboat moved slowly up the Nile. It had two large brown sails. When the wind died down, men got out on the bank and pulled the boat upstream.

By four o'clock that afternoon flocks of ibis were beginning to circle above the trees. There were ten to twenty birds in each flock. Theodore looked for his father. He found Mr. Roosevelt talking with one of the Egyptian sailors.

"Can't we tie up now, Father? This is the best chance I'll ever have to get an ibis." Teddy spoke quickly, eagerly.

Mr. Roosevelt smiled at his son. "I've already given the order. But we'll be in Egypt for several months. You have plenty of time."

"There are so many different kinds of birds, Father," said Teddy impatiently. "I must get a male and a female of each kind. They're for our museum. Lots of people can't come to Egypt to see these wonderful birds. So I have to get some really good ones to show them back home."

"I'm glad you're not hunting big animals. There wouldn't be any room left for us on the boat," said Mr. Roosevelt.

"When I'm grown I'm coming back to Africa and hunt elephants," said Teddy. "This trip I want birds."

"Well, we're about to tie up to those trees. I never knew ibis made so much noise. And I thought they were water birds."

"They are water birds, but the Egyptian ibis likes to follow a man plowing and pick up insects," Teddy told his father. "They are like herons. They wade in shallow water to fish. They roost in trees. That's strange for a water bird, but you can see them doing it right over there."

The top of a tree near the bank was whitened by the birds perched on the limbs. As the houseboat was pulled to the bank, a flock chattered noisily. Then it flew away.

"I don't want just any ibis," Teddy said. "I want them two feet long with an eight-inch bill. I want ones with black and white feathers."

"Are you going to measure them before you shoot?" Mr. Roosevelt pretended to be very serious.

Teddy laughed. "I'll just pick out big ones," he admitted, "and hope for the best. But I want fine specimens for our museum."

A MESSY CABIN

"Elliott, you haven't eaten a thing," said Mrs. Roosevelt that night.

"I wasn't hungry," Elliott answered. "Father, may I see you for a moment? Alone?"

"Of course." Mr. Roosevelt nodded to his younger son. He got up from the table.

132

When they were on deck, Elliott said, "Father, could I have a room by myself? I mean a cabin?"

"What's the matter? Have you and Theodore quarreled or fought with each other?"

"No, sir. Teddy's all right. But when he's doing something, that's all he thinks about. Now he's getting specimens for that museum of his."

"I'm glad he is," Mr. Roosevelt answered. "I want him to be outdoors. One reason we came to Egypt was to help his asthma."

"I wish he'd stay outdoors," said Elliott. "Father, come look at our cabin."

Mr. Roosevelt went with him to the cabin. Inside the small room he looked around in surprise. "I see what you mean," he said.

A large ibis was stretched out on the floor. Teddy's shotgun was on one bunk. Bottles of alcohol and acid were scattered about. The sharp smell of strong soap and alcohol gave the room an unpleasant odor.

"Teddy says he must go right back to work. He says the bird will be ruined if he doesn't stuff it tonight. I came down for just a few minutes before dinner, and I got half sick."

Teddy came into the cabin. He stopped in surprise at seeing his father. "Good evening, Father. Did you want me?" He looked suspiciously at Elliott.

"I never saw a messier cabin, Theodore. I wish you'd learn to be neat."

"I haven't time, Father. I get everything out, and then I have to work fast on my specimen. That's important."

Mr. Roosevelt sighed. "I'm glad to see you so interested, but it's hard on everyone else. Especially Elliott. He can't sleep here tonight."

"I'll clean it up when I'm through," Teddy promised his father.

"Let's go on deck, Elliott," said Mr. Roosevelt. "You can get your clothes later."

"Why don't you come on deck, too, Teddy?" asked Elliott. "Let's get that sailor to show us how to tie some more knots."

"I'd like to, Ellie, but I can't," said Teddy firmly. "I have to finish fixing up this ibis before I do anything else."

A MESSY ICEBOX

A month later Teddy was hunting on marshy ground. It was getting dark, but he thought he had seen a white-tailed plover. He had read about this rare bird, but he had never seen one.

"I must have one," he told himself.

The rushes came up to his waist. He bent down to hide himself as he slushed through the mud. He stepped into shallow water.

A brown bird with a white tail started running in the shallow water. Suddenly it rose into the air, its black and white wings beating swiftly.

Teddy lifted his shotgun. He was trembling with excitement.

He fired.

"The bird I wanted most of all," said Teddy, "and I missed."

He heard a bird crying *"Wh-ill, wh-ill."* Quickly he turned. As a second plover arose, Teddy aimed and fired. The bird fell. Shotgun in hand, Teddy waded out into the lake. He must get there before the bird sank under the water. He scooped the plover up and waded back to the bank. Then he hurried, with water dripping from his clothes, back to the houseboat.

Mrs. Roosevelt was waiting for him. "Goodness, Theodore! You're wet all over. Change your clothes quickly. Dinner is ready."

"But, Mother, I have a white-tailed plover. I have to get him ready first."

"No, you haven't," said Mrs. Roosevelt sternly. "You must get ready for dinner right now."

Teddy didn't argue. He turned to go to his cabin, but he worried that his unusual bird might spoil.

He went quietly and quickly to the kitchen. He lifted the icebox lid and placed the bird carefully where it would stay cool. After thinking a moment, he pulled a desert rat out of his pocket and placed it beside the plover. Then he hurried to change his clothes.

When dinner was nearly over Bamie said, "I need some more ice in my tea, Mother."

Mrs. Roosevelt rang for the Egyptian waiter. She asked him to bring the ice.

A minute later there was a loud, frightened yell from the kitchen. Mr. Roosevelt got up quickly. He disappeared into the kitchen.

When he came back he asked sternly, "Who put a dead rat in the icebox?"

Teddy looked up. "I did. That's a valuable rat, Father. He has black stripes on his back."

"He's still a rat, Theodore. We can't have you putting such things with our food."

"Oh, Theodore!" said his mother sadly. "Now I'll have to throw all that food away."

"He didn't hurt the food," Teddy said. "He couldn't have. He's dead."

"I couldn't eat it," said Mrs. Roosevelt. "I'd keep remembering the rat. Theodore, don't you ever think of anything but your collection?"

"Yes, Mother. But I had to put my plover in a cool, safe place." Teddy knew he was right. His tone was patient but certain. "You wouldn't want a really rare specimen ruined, would you?"

Mrs. Roosevelt looked hopelessly at her husband. "Theodore is the most determined child I've ever known. I'm sorry he ever learned how to shoot."

Mr. Roosevelt's eyes twinkled. "I had to get another cabin for Elliott. Maybe I'll have to get another houseboat for us."

The Literary Club

In the spring Mr. Roosevelt went back to New York on business. Mrs. Roosevelt and Bamie were visiting relatives in England. Theodore, Elliott, and Corinne were staying in Dresden, Germany, in order to learn German.

They were living with the Minckwitz family. For six days a week they were allowed to speak only German.

On Wednesdays they could speak English, and their cousins, Johnnie and Maud Elliott, came to spend the entire day with them.

One Wednesday afternoon in May 1873, Teddy and Johnnie were boxing in Teddy's room.

Maud, Corinne, and Elliott were sitting on a bench, watching.

"Now I have you," panted Teddy. He forced Johnnie into one corner of the roped-off boxing ring.

Johnnie sprang out. He struck quickly.

Teddy felt a sharp pain under his left eye. He struck back. He hit Johnnie on the nose.

"Time's up," Elliott yelled.

"Gee!" Teddy was panting. "That was a great round!"

Maud Elliott looked disgustedly at the two boys. "You're always boxing or wrestling," she said, "but I think Richard Minckwitz can throw either of you."

"You're almost as good, Teddy," said Johnnie admiringly.

"Richard's fun to wrestle with," said Teddy.

"Well, it's no fun to watch you," Maud argued. "We're allowed to speak English just one day, Teddy, and you want to box or wrestle. You can do that any day."

"Maud's right, Teddy," said Corinne.

"What would you like to do?" Teddy asked. "I thought you liked to watch us, Conie."

Corinne started to nod in agreement. Maud caught her eye. Corinne flushed. "No, I don't."

"Then what do you want to do?" Teddy asked again. "You didn't answer my question."

"We'd like to start a literary club," Maud said. "Conie writes poetry, and I like to write, too. We could read aloud each piece we wrote."

"Yes," said Corinne eagerly, "and we could copy each one into a notebook. I'll bet Aunt Anna would buy it."

Teddy looked at the two boys. They had nothing to say. He looked at the girls. They were leaning forward.

"All right," he said. "Let's try it. Each one will have to write something every week."

"I'll buy the notebook," said Maud. "We can call ourselves the Dresden Literary Club."

Teddy objected quickly. "We're Americans. Let's say Dresden Literary American Club."

Maud and Corinne agreed. They were delighted to have any name, if the boys would talk more and fight less.

"ALIVE AND KICKING"

The next Wednesday each one had written something. Corinne read a poem. All agreed it was good enough to go into the notebook.

Teddy read a scientific account of the habits of the Egyptian ibis.

Johnnie protested. "I'd just as soon you read the dictionary. Rather, in fact. I don't know what half those words mean."

"You don't know anything about natural history," retorted Teddy.

142

"And I'm not interested in learning," said Johnnie firmly.

Maud spoke up quickly. "I think we ought to have a little about each one of us in the note-book. Listen to this paragraph I've written about Theodore:

'I must tell you something about Theodore. You know he was a naturalist on a small scale. He was a very amusing boy, but he had a great fault. He was very absent-minded, so much so that when ever his mother would tell him to go and do something for her he would say, 'Oh yes, you pretty little thing,' but instead of doing it directly he would go and skin his birds, and then he always thought he could do things better than anyone else.

Signed, MAUD ELLIOTT—Aged 11'"

"You make me sound as though I were dead," Teddy protested. "I'm alive and kicking. I'm kicking especially about that last sentence."

"That's perfect," said Elliott. "Maud has Ted-

dy down pat. Let's put that in the notebook. Her piece is really good."

"What about my piece on the ibis?" asked Teddy.

"I vote no," said Johnnie.

"No," said Maud and Elliott together.

Corinne didn't vote. "I know you can do one that'll get in, Teddy. You can do things better than most people," she said comfortingly.

144

For the next week Teddy had very little time to wrestle with Elliott or with Richard Minckwitz. He had no time to go hunting. As soon as his lessons were finished, he would go back to his room and work on a piece for the notebook.

He couldn't decide what to write. After thinking of various subjects, he began writing about General Washington winning the Battle of Yorktown. That was an important battle, and Teddy knew enough about it to write on it.

He read over what he had written. "This won't do," he thought. "Maud and Conie aren't interested in soldiers and battles. Neither is Johnnie. They won't listen."

On Monday he thought of a good subject. He'd write about animals as if they were people. Excitedly he began to write.

When the Dresden Literary American Club met on Wednesday, Teddy was ready. He had his story in his hands. "I want to read first," he said. "If you don't like this, I can't ever please the Dresden Literary American Club."

"Everybody quiet," said Johnnie. "We'll see if Teddy can write anything worth listening to."

Teddy adjusted his glasses and stood up. This is the story he read:

MRS. FIELD MOUSE'S DINNER PARTY

BY THEODORE ROOSEVELT—AGED FOURTEEN

"My dear," said Mrs. M. to Mr. M. one day as they were sitting on an elegant acorn sofa, just after breakfast. "My dear, I think that we must give a dinner party."

"A what, my love?" exclaimed Mr. M. in a surprised tone.

"A dinner party," returned Mrs. M. firmly. "You have no objections, I suppose?"

"Of course not, of course not," said Mr. M. hastily, for there was a stern look in his wife's eye. "But why have it yet for a while, my love?"

146

"Why indeed! That's a pretty question! After that hateful Mrs. Frog's great tea party the other evening." Mrs. M. covered her eyes and fell into hysterics.

Of course Mr. M. had to promise to have it whenever she liked.

"Then the day after tomorrow would not be too early?"

Mr. M. tried to protest, but Mrs. M. did not heed him. She continued: "You can get the cheese and bread from Squeak, Nibble & Co. The other things you can get from the firm of Brown Mouse & Wood Rats."

"But in such a short——" commenced Mr. M.

Mrs. M. cut him off sharply. "You're always raising objections. We will have it the day after tomorrow. I hear that Mr. Chipmunk has in a new supply of nuts. You can get some of them. And arrange with Messrs. Gloworm and Firefly to provide the lamps for the party.

"Tommy Crickett can carry around the invitations," Mrs. M. continued. "We'll have our cousins, the Mice and the Rats. Then we'll have Sir Lizard, Mr. Chipmunk, Mr. and Mrs. Bullfrog, Miss Katydid, Mr. and Mrs. Grasshopper, Lord Beetle, Mr. Ant, Sir Butterfly, Mr. Bee, Mr. Wasp, Mr. Hornet, Lady Maybug, and a number of others."

Mr. M. meekly got his hat and went off.

Water Bug & Co. conveyed everything to Shady Nook, the home of Mr. and Mrs. Mouse. On the night of the party the whole family in their best dresses waited for the visitors.

The first visitor to arrive was Lady Maybug. Mrs. Mouse said to herself, "She's a stupid old thing, always first." Aloud she said, "How charming to see you, Lady Maybug! I can always rely on your being on time."

"Yes, Ma'am, but it is so hot," said Lady Maybug. "And my carriage almost broke down."

She sat down heavily on the sofa. The sofa had one weak leg. Lady Maybug was no lightweight. The sofa fell over, pitching Lady Maybug to the floor with a great thud.

Mrs. M. went to help her. So did Tommy Crickett. Tommy was to be the waiter and was dressed in new red trousers.

Just as they got Lady Maybug up, the doorbell rang.

Tommy hurried to the door. "Nibble, Squeak & Co.," he announced in a shrill piping voice.

Mrs. Mouse shot a daggerlike glance at him.

"Mr. Squeak and Mr. Nibble, Ma'am," said Tommy hastily.

In a few minutes the guests came pouring in. Mrs. Mouse quickly called the party in to dinner, for the cook had boiled the hickory nuts too long. They would spoil if not served immediately.

Mrs. M. had invited one person too many for the plates. Mr. M. had to do without one. At first this was not noticed, as each person was seeing who could get the most to eat.

After a while Sir Lizard turned round and remarked, "Er, I say, Mr. M., why don't you take something to eat?"

"Mr. M. is not at all hungry tonight, are you, my dear?" put in Mrs. M., smiling at Sir Lizard, then frowning at Mr. M.

"Not at all, not at all," replied Mr. M. hastily.

Sir Lizard seemed about to continue, but Mrs. M. rang for the dessert.

There was a sort of struggling noise in the kitchen, but that was the only answer. A second ring, no answer. A third ring.

In dashed the unlucky Tommy Crickett with the cheese. But alas! When halfway in the room, his beautiful new red trousers came down. Tommy and the cheese rolled straight into Miss Dragon Fly, who fainted without delay.

Tommy's howls made the room ring. There

was confusion until Tommy was kicked out of the room and Miss Dragon Fly was revived.

Miss Katydid's little sister broke in with a sharp squeak. "Katy kissed Mr. Woodmouse!"

"Katy didn't," returned her brother.

"Katy did."

"Katy didn't."

Miss Katydid blushed crimson, but she was saved when the lamps suddenly commenced to burn blue.

Mrs. M. gave a glance at Mr. M. which made him quake in his shoes. "There, Mr. M.! Now see what you have done!" said the lady of the house sternly.

"My dear, I told you Messrs. Gloworm and Firefly couldn't get enough oil. You had the party too soon. It was your own fault," said Mr. M., worked up to desperation.

As the room was getting dark, the company left with some abruptness and confusion.

When they were gone, Mrs. M. gave her husband a glance that would have smashed three millstones of moderate size. By the light of one bed lamp, she turned an eagle eye on Mr. M. and said——

But we will now draw a curtain over the scene that followed, and say, "Good-by."

After Teddy had finished reading the story, Corinne said delightedly, "There! I told you Teddy could do it. I'll bet that story gets in the notebook."

"I'll say it does," said Johnnie.

"Me, too," said Elliott. "But I know Teddy. I'd better correct the spelling."

"Teddy, why don't you be a writer when you grow up?" asked Maud.

"I am going to write," said Teddy, "but I'm going to do a lot of other things, too."

Lightweight Champion

Soon after his return to New York City from Germany, Teddy started taking boxing lessons from Mr. John Long. Mrs. Roosevelt didn't want her son to learn how to fight from a professional boxer. But Teddy said, "Mother, I still remember how those two boys threw me around on the stagecoach. You wouldn't want that to happen again—especially not now, when I'm fifteen years old."

"No, I wouldn't," said Mrs. Roosevelt. "I suppose you should be able to defend yourself."

She talked with Mr. Cutler, Teddy's new tutor. Arthur Cutler had been hired to teach all the children, but especially to prepare Teddy to enter Harvard University.

"I think you'd better let him learn to box, Mrs. Roosevelt," said Mr. Cutler. "He wants to do it, and it will be good for him. He does extremely well in anything he wants to do. He's even working hard on mathematics now, though he doesn't like it."

After her talk with Mr. Cutler, Mrs. Roosevelt agreed to allow Teddy to begin the boxing lessons with Mr. Long.

Mr. Long's gymnasium was in an old building on Broadway. There were pictures of famous prize fighters on the walls. Along the wall were punching bags. In the center of the room was a square boxing ring, marked off by ropes.

The first day Mr. Long boxed with Teddy.

Mr. Long had been a lightweight champion. Now he weighed 160 pounds. Theodore weighed just under 130 pounds. He had short arms.

Without his glasses he was very nearsighted. He had grown stronger. He no longer had asthma. Now he was intent on building up his body.

Mr. Long tied on the boxing gloves. Then he went to the center of the ring. "Hit me, Teddy," he said.

Teddy started a quick left swing, stopped it, and swung hard with his right.

"That's good," said Mr. Long. He had stopped the right swing with his glove. "That would fool lots of men. Very few would have been prepared for such a quick change. But your eyes gave it away."

"How?" asked Teddy.

"Your eyes weren't looking where your left hand hit. They were looking where you meant to hit with your right hand. You'll get over doing that. You'll be a good fighter. Now try again to hit me, Teddy."

Teddy practiced hard, just as he worked hard

on mathematics. He learned to hit clean and straight. He became very angry when anyone hit him below the belt.

"It doesn't matter what the other fellow does," said Mr. Long. "You must fight your own fight."

"It does matter," argued Teddy. "When I'm right, I know it."

Mr. Long shook his head. "One thing I'll say for you. You never try to take unfair advantage of the other fellow. And, if you can help it, you won't let the other fellow get away with being unfair to you."

FOR ALL THE PEOPLE

One day in October Teddy was punching the bag in Mr. Long's gymnasium. He heard the sound of a drum. Then he heard the entire band.

Teddy went to a window. "What's that?" he asked the man next to him.

"That's a political marching club," the man answered. "There's an election next month. We must elect the mayor, the governor, and the President of the United States."

Mr. Long had come up silently. He tapped Teddy on the shoulder. "Those men run street-cars and busses, work in factories, and labor with their hands. Much of what they know they learned by selling newspapers as boys."

"I've learned a lot at the Newsboys' Lodging-house," Teddy said. "I have some good friends there."

"Oh," said Mr. Long, "I didn't know you went there."

"I go there once a month when I'm in New York," Teddy answered. "Until a boy named Mike Brady left for a job on a ranch out west, I went there every week."

A short, dark boy spoke up. "That's not the only place he goes, Mr. Long. He's teaching my kid brothers to write English—every Tuesday night, at Miss Slattery's School. She has special classes for Italians."

Teddy looked at the younger boy. "You must be Tony Antonelli. I have three Antonelli boys in my class."

"Yes, I'm Tony," said the dark boy. "You run for mayor and I'll vote for you."

"Thanks, Tony. I'll be seeing you." Teddy walked along with Mr. Long.

"You see," said Mr. Long, "the men we saw in the parade elect the men who govern us."

"That's right. They do. They're the real people of this country," said Teddy. "When I'm twenty-one, I'm going to join just such a group. I'm no snob. I want to be with the people—all kinds of people. They all go together to make up America."

"Young people like you will build a great country, too," replied Mr. Long.

Although he had short arms, Teddy became a good boxer. His thin chest was growing thicker and stronger. When Mr. Long offered a pewter cup for the championship in each weight, Teddy entered for the lightweight championship.

"I'll go to the matches with you," Mr. Cutler offered. "I'll be your second. I'll see you have a lemon to suck on between rounds."

"I wish you would," Teddy answered.

At the gymnasium he changed to boxing shorts and shoes. His fingers trembled as he tied the shoelaces. "I'm getting nervous," he confessed.

"So is your opponent," Mr. Cutler replied.

Teddy felt better as he thought of that.

At the ring Mr. Long greeted him. "Good luck, Teddy! You're fighting Dick Williams."

Teddy looked at his opponent. Dick was thin and tall. "He's faster than I am," he told Mr. Cutler. "I'm going to attack all the time."

During the fight Teddy kept moving forward. He jabbed constantly with his left hand. Dick didn't like it. He kept drawing back. Teddy never had a chance to hit him very hard, but he hit Dick often.

He won that fight. He won his next two matches, too.

The fourth match was for the championship. It was to go four rounds.

John Hart was taller than Teddy. His arms were longer. It would be a tough fight.

For two rounds the boys were even. The bell rang to end the second round.

Teddy dropped his hands to his sides, but John had started a long swing. He didn't hear the bell. The blow caught Teddy full on the nose.

"Foul!" shouted the spectators. "Foul!"

Teddy had seen John Hart's eyes. He knew that John had not meant to foul him.

His nose ached from the blow. But Teddy lifted his right arm to attract attention. "Quiet! He didn't mean to do it," he told the spectators. "John didn't hear the bell."

The booing stopped. Teddy went to his corner of the ring.

Mr. Cutler bathed Teddy's nose in cold water. "You play fair yourself," he said, "and when you know the other fellow means to play fair, you stand up for him. That's what I like about you. Now go out and win this fight."

"I do want to win the cup," said Teddy.

He boxed well. At the end of the fourth round, Mr. Long raised Teddy's hand, to show he was the winner.

The Bull Moose

It was a raw, cold November day. Teddy was seventeen on October 27, and for a birthday present Mr. Roosevelt had given him a moose-hunting trip in northern Maine.

The hunter Bill Sewall was his guide. For four days Mr. Sewall and Teddy had hunted, but they had shot nothing larger than a grouse.

"I have today and tomorrow to get a moose," said Teddy, warming his hands and gloves over the campfire. "We haven't even seen one."

Bill Sewall looked up at the rising sun. "Be patient," he advised. "The moose is the biggest and noblest of all the deer family. Naturally it's the hardest to kill."

Teddy thought for a moment. "I've killed only one deer, and that was at night," he said. "When we went caribou hunting on snowshoes last February, at least I saw a caribou. I saw it leap over some fallen tree trunks, but I didn't have time to shoot. And I never saw it again."

"Did you enjoy that trip?" asked Bill Sewall.

"Yes, I did," Teddy answered honestly. "The snowy forest was beautiful, and we had some fine times. But when I go out hunting for caribou, I want to get a caribou."

Mr. Sewall looked through the birch trees at the slowly rising sun. "We can see well enough to start," he decided. "Remember, a moose can be dangerous. If you wound one, it may turn and charge you."

"The only thing I'm afraid of is not seeing a moose at all," answered Teddy.

Mr. Sewall poured a bucket of water on the fire. "Make sure your rifle is all right, and let's get going," he said.

They walked quickly through the forest. They came to a part where all the trees had been cut.

"We won't find any game here," said Mr. Sewall disgustedly. "Whoever did this cutting cut everything down because it was cheaper than just getting out the big trees. It will be years before the timber grows back."

"But that's foolish." Teddy was indignant. "If we don't save our forests, we won't have any lumber, or any game either. This is criminal waste."

"I'll show you worse than this when we go back to town," promised Mr. Sewall. "There's a big factory there which has poisoned the river. It kills every salmon that comes from the ocean up the river to lay its eggs."

Teddy stopped. He surveyed the wasted land.

"We must learn better," he said with deep feeling. "Some of the land should belong to all the people. There should be national parks. Certainly the rivers should be kept pure. We have to protect our forests and streams and minerals—all our natural resources."

"We can't do anything about it today," said Mr. Sewall. He approved of Teddy's concern, but he wanted to get back into the forest as quickly as possible.

They tramped slowly forward over the marshy ground. Beyond the brown, grassy marsh was a pine forest, but even here they found walking was difficult. Their feet slipped on the mud. Water sloshed up on their boots. They stayed within the forest, so that they would not be seen.

After an hour of hard going, they came to some young trees. Bill Sewall pointed at one that was bent over. "A moose straddled that one and rode it to the ground," he said.

Teddy saw that on other trees the bark had been peeled away. A moose had cut the bark as high as he could reach with his sharp teeth. The bent tree had most of the tender top eaten out.

"Moose did that this morning," Sewall whispered. He walked silently to the edge of the woods.

Teddy followed. He was tense with excitement. Perhaps their bad luck was over.

Mr. Sewall dropped to his knees. He pointed straight ahead.

Teddy stared. A huge black moose was walking with great strides through the marsh. It had long legs and a big head. Antlers as big as shovels were held back against its shoulders.

Stepping quickly forward, Teddy raised his rifle to his shoulder.

Mr. Sewall shook his head. The moose's body

was partly hidden by bushes and the brown marsh grass.

Disappointed, Teddy lowered the rifle. The bull moose was too far away for a good shot. It made a splendid picture of strength and nobility as it stood erect. Its fine head was thrown back. Its deep chest parted the marsh grass.

Teddy breathed deeply. "Golly! If I had to be an animal, I'd like to be a bull moose. That's the noblest animal of them all."

"Come on," whispered Sewall. "It's finished breakfast. It won't go far unless we scare it."

Mr. Sewall and Teddy stayed near the edge of the woods. Walking quickly, they kept about even with the moose. Occasionally Teddy saw the dark animal trotting through the marsh.

Once it stopped to look around suspiciously. Mr. Sewall halted abruptly. Teddy waited anxiously. "If we've scared it, I'll never see it again," he thought hopelessly.

The huge moose raised its antlers high in the air. It lifted one hind leg and scratched its neck.

Teddy felt little pinpricks of hope and fear make goose flesh on his arms.

Bill Sewall pointed. "Maybe it will go to that thicket of little spruce trees," he said in a low, tense voice.

They watched the moose wander about. Then it chose a point where there were some thick bushes. The moose shuffled to its knees and lay down.

Sewall whispered in Teddy's ear, "The moose hasn't seen us. It will be watching the trail it made." He dropped to his hands and knees and began to crawl.

Teddy crawled behind him. The ground was soft and wet. It made a slight sucking noise as he moved forward. Where the ground was higher Mr. Sewall dropped down and wriggled along on his stomach.

This was hard work, Teddy discovered. His arms and shoulders began to ache from the effort of pulling himself along. His wet knees and legs were very cold. His rifle kept getting in his way.

They crawled to a tiny hill. "Here," said Mr. Sewall. He barely breathed the word.

Teddy wriggled up beside him. The air was still. The grass was motionless. "Where?" he whispered.

The guide pointed. Teddy peered cautiously at the thicket of young spruce. He pushed his rifle gently forward. "I can't see a thing," he said to himself. "It's gone. There! What's that?"

Teddy saw a slow, regular motion. "Why, that's its big ears," he told himself. The moose was lazily moving its ears.

Mr. Sewall touched Teddy on the shoulder. "I'm ready," whispered Teddy, bringing his rifle close against his shoulder.

Teddy felt the blood throbbing in his temples. His heart was beating fast. "I should have cleaned my glasses," he thought suddenly. But he could see well enough, and his muscles were steady.

Bill Sewall pulled a dry twig from his pocket. He snapped it loudly between his fingers.

The moose's ears stopped flapping. For a moment everything was still.

Then the moose rose nimbly to its feet. One moment it was on the ground. The next moment it was on its feet, ready to run.

The moose stood broadside to Teddy, its huge body black against the light. Its large antlers were lifted. Columns of gray steam rose from its nostrils. Slowly, stiffly, it turned its head toward the hunters.

Teddy aimed carefully, just behind the enormous shoulder. He squeezed the trigger. The gun roared.

The moose reared up on its hind legs. It gave a tremendous leap. Blood sprang from the nostrils of the wounded moose.

The moose wheeled and began to walk slowly toward Teddy. Its antlers beat against the young spruce that stood in its way. The moose saw or smelled the boy lying on the ground watching it. Suddenly it gave a loud, bellowing roar.

The moose charged.

Teddy aimed between the eyes. Quickly but steadily he pulled the trigger.

The moose leaped high. It snorted with pain and anger. Then slowly the long legs collapsed. The moose tumbled forward. It was dead before it hit the ground.

"Whew!" said Teddy.

"That was close," said Mr. Sewall. He got up slowly. "One more second, and I'd have shot it myself."

Teddy scrambled to his feet. "I'm glad you didn't."

"So am I," Bill Sewall agreed. "But I've seen a moose break a wolf's back with just one blow of its forelegs. What took you so long?"

"I wanted to be sure I'd kill it," said Teddy.

"We'll have moose steak tonight." Mr. Sewall bent down to examine the huge, broad antlers. "I suppose you'll have the head and horns fixed up when you get back to New York—so that you can hang them on the wall?"

"No, sir. I'm going to do every speck of the work myself. That head goes in the Roosevelt Museum of Natural History."

"It's a job I don't want," said Mr. Sewall. "You're welcome to it."

"It *is* messy," admitted Teddy, "but I don't mind. I shot him myself, and I'll stuff the head myself. When I start a job, I intend to finish it."

All-Round American

It was October 26, 1958. Eight boys were in the clubroom of the Boy Scout Moose Patrol. They ranged in age from twelve to fifteen. The oldest boy, the patrol leader, suddenly cupped his hands around his lips. He gave the loud, trumpeting call of a bull moose.

"That'll tell 'em something is about to start," said the assistant patrol leader. "You make the pictures on the wall rattle with that call."

"I mean to. This skit tomorrow must be the best ever given in this town. Everybody will be there to honor Teddy Roosevelt. We'll give the skit. Then we'll go out and plant our Theodore Roosevelt Memorial Beech tree on the school grounds."

"If he were still living, he'd be one hundred years old tomorrow."

A small, slim boy walked over to one corner and looked admiringly at the straight young beech. Its roots in a ball of dirt were wrapped in moist burlap. "We picked a beauty," he said. "I just hope it lives."

"It must live," said another boy. "When he was president, Teddy Roosevelt worked hard to save our forests and preserve our wild life. He believed in the conservation of our natural resources."

"That's a mouthful," said the slim boy, "but I know——"

The patrol leader interrupted. "Wait a minute, Harry. Let's go through our parts. We're going to show what an all-round American Theodore Roosevelt was. In order to do that, each of you seven will act like him at one time of his life. Every now and then I will put in a few words. Now, Harry, right after I give the call, what happens?"

"I rush on the stage—like this. I have boxing gloves and trunks on. I have a book under my arm—see. I'm Teddy Roosevelt when he was a student at Harvard University. Then Bill comes out and we box. I knock Bill out. That shows how strong I've made myself. Then I recite a poem. That shows I like books."

Bill stood up. "I don't believe Harry can knock me out. Let's see."

"Teddy Roosevelt could have," answered Harry. "He led a strenuous life, as a boy and as a man. Tomorrow I'm Teddy the athlete."

The two boys began to box. They weren't hitting hard, but suddenly Harry shot through a right to the chin. "See!" he shouted. "That's the way Teddy did it. You can't whip Teddy."

The patrol leader stopped them. "That part's fine," he said. "Let's go ahead with the rehearsal. Next we have to show why the Moose Patrol was picked to give this skit."

"I do that," said another boy. "I'm Teddy now —when he was a hunter." This boy was dressed in buckskin hunting clothes. He picked up a .22 rifle. He began crawling on the floor.

Two boys pushed a cardboard bull moose along one side of the wall. The moose was huge and black. It looked real.

"We did a good job when we built that," said the assistant patrol leader.

The "hunter" crawled forward. He aimed carefully. He squeezed the trigger. The gun roared. The moose fell over.

"I have some more blank cartridges," said the hunter. "Boy, this is a lot easier than hitting a rabbit or a squirrel! Every time I shoot, that moose falls dead."

The patrol leader grinned. "We see to that," he said. "At this point I tell how Teddy Roosevelt hunted bull moose and grizzly bears in the Rocky Mountains, and lions and elephants in Africa. He liked big game that could put up a fight. He liked the danger and excitement. He didn't kill just for the fun of killing."

"He brought back unusual specimens for our museums," interrupted a studious-looking boy. "He was always interested in natural history. Once, when he was running for president, someone asked him how he felt. 'I feel as fit as a bull moose,' Teddy answered."

"We've included that in our skit," said the patrol leader, "because that's why his political party was called the Bull Moose party. Now who's next?"

"I am," answered the studious-looking boy. He was dressed in a cowboy suit, with large spurs. "I'm Teddy when he was a rancher. Wait a minute now till I tell you. Teddy wrote a lot of books on ranching and hunting. I've read several of them and they're great. He said all a man had to do was to shoot as accurately at a lion or a rhinoceros as he would at a soda-pop bottle. That takes nerve."

The "hunter" scrambled to his feet. "You know what I think? I think Teddy had a lot of luck."

"He thought so, too," said the "rancher." "But he earned his luck. He had troubles and sorrows, too. He was in the New York legislature and fighting hard for honest government when his mother and his wife died in the same week. He went to North Dakota and bought a ranch. That's where I come in."

As each boy acted his part, he tried to speak and act as Teddy would have. The "rancher" got up and walked heavily toward the center of the room. He took off his glasses. He rubbed

182

his eyes wearily. "I've been in the saddle forty straight hours, and not a wink of sleep. This rounding up cattle is rough work."

The assistant patrol leader approached him. "You want something?" he asked.

"Just a bed for the night," answered "Teddy."

A tall, heavy boy swaggered toward him. He wore rough clothes and carried a pistol in a holster. "Look at the tenderfoot," he said. "Hey, Four-eyes! Dance!"

"Teddy the rancher" looked around in bewilderment. The tough boy yanked his pistol out. "I said *dance.* Now *dance!*" He aimed the pistol near "Teddy's" foot. "Hurry up! Dance!" He pulled the trigger.

"Teddy" danced. But he kept edging closer to the bully. A shot would ring out. "Teddy" would jump. But he moved closer and closer. Suddenly "Teddy" lashed out with his right hand. With his left hand he caught hold of the pistol.

The bully fell heavily backward.

"Teddy" stood calmly over him. "Now get out of town," he said. "I like peace, but I'm ready to fight for it any time I have to."

The boy on the floor rubbed his chin. "Don't hit so hard next time, Ed," he protested. "This is just acting."

Ed grinned. "I thought I was Teddy. That's what gave me strength."

"Teddy didn't stay out west," said the patrol leader. "He came back east and got into politics. He got to be assistant secretary of the navy a couple of years before the Spanish-American War started."

A boy in a dark-blue suit moved to one side of the room. From behind a screen, a gray cardboard battleship mounted on tiny wheels was pushed into the room. Another boy fixed a target on the opposite wall. The battleship began firing. Its little cannon exploded loudly.

"Our sailors can't shoot," said the boy who was acting the part of Theodore Roosevelt, assistant secretary of the navy. "They must learn how. We must have this fleet ready for war. The Spaniards are cruel to the Cubans. The Cubans are our neighbors. Before long we'll have to fight for them."

The patrol leader announced, "That war started in 1898. The American fleet met the Spanish fleet."

A second gray battleship rolled across the room. The American battleship opened fire. A moment later the Spanish ship exploded.

Now a boy in a soldier's khaki uniform strode toward the center of the room. "I didn't get to see that sea battle," he said, speaking as Colonel Theodore Roosevelt. "I wanted to fight. So I organized the Rough Riders. We had cowboys and hunters and college men. We were sent to help Cuba."

The assistant patrol leader walked forward. He had put on a military overcoat and military cap. "Colonel Roosevelt," he said.

"Yes, General."

"I watched you lead the charge up San Juan Hill. You handled your men magnificently. On a field where many men were brave, you were the bravest."

"Colonel Roosevelt" saluted. "Thank you, General," he said. "But my men did the work. They deserve the credit."

The patrol leader held up a teddy bear. "Teddy Roosevelt became a national hero. This toy bear was named for him. Lots of boys were named for him. He was elected governor of New York."

A stout boy came forward. He was well dressed, and he had pasted a black mustache on his upper lip. He acted the part of Teddy Roosevelt, governor of New York.

"Good morning, Governor," a short boy with a false beard said to him.

"Good morning, Senator. You wanted to see me?" said "Governor Roosevelt."

"Yes, Governor. I'm disturbed about the way you're running this state. You have every wealthy man in New York down on you." The "senator" was speaking angrily. "It must stop. You can't fight the railroads, the banks, and the people."

"Governor Roosevelt" interrupted him. "The people are behind me," he declared sternly. "I promised them an honest government. They know I'm giving it to them. What's more, they like it." He pointed a finger at the "senator's" chest. "Those who don't like it are dishonest."

"No man can call me dishonest," snapped the "senator," "and get away with it. You'll never be elected to an office in New York again."

The patrol leader spoke up. "He could have been, very easily. But he was needed for a bigger job. In 1900 he was elected vice president of the United States. A few months later President McKinley was shot. He died soon after, and Theodore Roosevelt was made president of the United States."

A fine-looking boy took the part of President Roosevelt. "I believe in a strong government," he said, "that will protect every citizen in this country. I'll fight against the wealthy man when he's evil, and fight for him when he's good. I'll do the same for a poor man. And I believe in standing by my friends. I've just appointed my newsboy friend Mike to be governor of Alaska, and he'll make a good governor."

One boy said, "You didn't give us a square deal. I'm from Colombia, in South America. You took Panama away from us."

"I had to do that and you know it. We had to build the Panama Canal," said "President Roosevelt" hotly. "We couldn't wait for ships to go all around South America. The trip took too long. It wasn't safe in time of war. It wasn't safe for you. It wasn't safe for the United States."

Then he added proudly, "Yes, we built the Panama Canal. It was well worth doing."

A second boy came forward. "You took my timber and my land," he accused the "president." "I'd have made a million dollars if it hadn't been for you."

"President Roosevelt" gazed sternly at the speaker. "You were robbing the people. You were destroying our natural resources. I saved the forests. I kept you from poisoning the rivers. I built up Yellowstone and Yosemite National Parks."

The man slunk away. "President Roosevelt" watched him go. "When a man like that attacks me, I know I've done some good in the world," he said. "Sometimes you have to fight strenuously as well as live strenuously. 'Speak softly,

but carry a big stick.' That's a good motto for any man, or any country."

A boy in a blue sailor suit came up to him. "You wanted to see me, President Roosevelt?"

"Yes, Admiral Evans. We've built up a fine navy, but very few nations realize it. I'm going to send our fleet around the world. If they see how great it is, they won't dare to attack us."

"Fighting Bob Evans" looked admiringly at the "president." "That's wonderful. Show 'em the big stick, and you may not have to use it."

"President Roosevelt" said, "Right! Get the ships ready. I want you to start soon."

The "admiral" nodded. "I'll bring them back in better shape than when we left," he promised, and turned away.

"I have tried to give the people a good and an honest government," said the "president." "I have helped to make and to keep peace in the world. I did more than anyone else to end the war between Russia and Japan. I believe our government should be strong, in order that every person, rich or poor, may have justice. And I have made it strong. I have worked to keep our wood and coal, our oil and minerals from being wasted away. I saw to it that the Panama Canal was built. But the thing I'm proudest of is this — I've seen to it that every person can get a square deal."'

All the boys cheered.